Books by M K Scott

Cupid's Catering Company
Culinary Cozy Mystery

Wedding Cake Blues
Truffle Me Not
Double Chocolate Deception

The Talking Dog Detective Agency
Cozy Mystery

A Bark in the Night
Requiem for a Rescue Dog Queen
Bark Twice for Danger
The Ghostly Howl
Dog Park Romeo
On St. Nick's Trail

The Painted Lady Inn Mysteries Series
Culinary Cozy Mystery

Murder Mansion
Drop Dead Handsome
Killer Review

Christmas Calamity

Death Pledges a Sorority

Caribbean Catastrophe

Weddings Can be Murder

The Skeleton Wore Diamonds

Death of a Honeymoon

Cakewalk to Murder

Sailors Take Warning

Two Many Sleuths

The Way Over the Hill Gang Series

Cozy Mystery

Late for Dinner

Late for Bingo

Late for Shuffleboard

Late for Square Dancing

Late for Love

Late for the Wedding (Dec 2021)

Two Many Sleuths Glossary

(There may be a few unfamiliar expressions for readers. Hopefully, the glossary will clear things up.)

Aces – really great to residents of the United Kingdom as opposed to a high value card. Ex: That's aces!

Across the Pond – across the Atlantic Ocean.

Anglophile – A person who greatly admires Britain/England.

Bloody – this is used instead of very by Brits. Example: Bloody terrific means very good.

Brilliant – this is usually a nod to brilliance. Similar to saying, "Great job," or "Genius." This is often used sarcastically by Brits to mean just the opposite.

Brit – nickname for a person from Britain.

CC Television – close circuit camera.

Constable – policeman. It's usually used in a friendly manner.

Chuff/Chuffed – is used to mean excited or pleased by Brits and Canadians, alike. It is also slang for butt, but not in this book.

Crikey – is a British exclamation of surprise, astonishment or wonder.

Cuppa – refers to a cup of tea. (British slang)

Lend a hand – help

Loo – bathroom/restroom.

Lovely – while this is normally compliment meaning beautiful or pleasing, it is often used sarcastically by Brits to mean just the opposite. The meaning can be determined by the speaker, tone, and situation.

Lush – while can mean heavy drinker, it is actually a compliment in the UK meaning pretty, beautiful or sexy. Lush is also used to mean large or luxurious.

Porter – someone who carries your luggage. Porters are more commonly associated with trains in the US. We usually use the term sky cap in the US.

RFID lifters – This is a person who can take advantage of radio frequency identification credit cards by using a device that records the frequency of the credit card by nearly being near the card holder. This is a big problem in international airports.

Snowbird Yankee – Someone North of the Mason Dixon Line who heads to the Southern states when the weather gets cold. They usually have a second home in the warmer states.

Spot of Trouble – Trouble, mischief, or bothersome issues. It usually implies something not disastrous.

Tickety boo – in good order. Fine.

War of Northern Aggression – This refers to the American Civil War and is commonly used by Southerners.

Yank – When used by folks from the United Kingdom, means American.

Two Many Sleuths

The Painted Lady Inn Mysteries

By

MK Scott

Chapter One

A WEEK WITHOUT a murder or the mention of any crime made Donna Tollhouse Taber grin. She adjusted the car window clamps on the British flags and stepped back, resting her hands on her lower back. "I think it's a nice touch."

Her detective husband, Mark, ran a hand through his salt and pepper hair. "I don't know." His face scrunched up. "It might be over the top. Howard doesn't strike me as the showy type. He keeps things low-key, a proper Brit."

Typical. Her husband thought he knew all about the neighbors over the pond due to having previously researched diamonds and jewel heists. He'd struck up an online relationship with a Scotland Yard Detective Inspector, Inspector Howard Dudley. Never mind that her husband hadn't put in the hours she had watching BBC mysteries and *The Great British Baking Show*. If Howard didn't appreciate her efforts to welcome them, his wife, Elizabeth, certainly would.

"A proper Brit might mention they don't go in for pomp and ceremony, but just look at the royal weddings. They go crazy about those," she informed him.

"Well, you'd know more about that than me. All I can hope for is a nice, quiet time with no murders. I told the station not to call me unless it's an emergency. A vacation is still a vacation even if I don't leave the state."

"The best thing to do is not answer your phone."

The Legacy Police Force numbered thirty-eight—six more than last year—but Donna still had doubts about her husband not getting pulled into a case. Surely, they could handle anything that came up on their own. Still—she gave her husband a loving perusal—Mark had solved eleven murders, with her help, of course. It's no wonder they'd need their help.

"Can't do that. It's not like I'm a stock boy, and when I'm missing, the green beans don't get shelved on time."

"I know." Before he could start his usual rant about a law enforcement officer being a public trust, she held up one hand. "I know it's an honor protecting the citizens of Legacy, but you need to let someone else do it."

"You're right," Mark agreed as he swung open the car door. "Let's go get our guests."

His phone rang on cue, and Donna recognized the station number. Her eyes rolled up, knowing the inevitable outcome.

Her husband answered the phone and muttered, "Sorry to hear that but I'm still on vacation. I have faith you can handle it."

Donna slid into her side of the car and popped her CD of favorite British ballads into the player before closing the door. She waited until her husband wiggled behind the steering wheel before asking, "What did they want?"

"Assistance on a case," he answered while backing out.

That much she could have guessed. "What kind of case?"

"Probable murder."

"Probable?" The word *probable* had little to do with *murder*. Premeditated, self-defense, and even accidental could pair up with murder. "What makes it probable?"

"Shot in the back of the head while gardening."

Good heavens! A person murdered while pulling weeds or deadheading roses. "How awful. Anyone I know?"

While all crimes should be regarded with horror and repulsion, knowing the victim made it somehow worse.

"Margery Baumgarten."

"Margery!" She pressed her hands over her heart. "I just saw her the other day at the Friends of the Library luncheon. She brought the tomato mozzarella salad. It could have done with a touch of dill, but I'm grateful I didn't mention it. I'd hate for that to be on her mind before being killed."

Mark put the car into drive. "It is just as well I'm not handling the case. It's always hard dealing with friends. Too many emotions can cloud your judgment."

"Well, we weren't super good friends. In a town the size of Legacy, I went to school with everyone my age. Sure, I do see Margery at many events."

A few blocks passed without talking while the strains of Barbara Allen swirled around them. The melancholic music got Donna thinking about Margery. They hadn't been good friends, but she knew of her and some of her trials. Her husband Jeff's wandering eye was known—at least to Donna. "Tell them to check out the husband."

"They always do," Mark answered without looking at her. "Standard procedure."

Donna harrumphed. Sure, all the police dramas looked at family members first. Enough cold cases illustrated forensic procedure that failed to nail down the case even when everyone knew the spouse should be charged. The facts only came out a few decades later: an eyewitness who saw something but was too scared to speak finally came forward, a piece of evidence was unearthed in the victim's former home by new owners, or a crackerjack detective decided to wade through the cold case files. She had a crackerjack detective sitting right beside her. However, Donna didn't discount her own personal strings that she could pull for information.

"I think you should do it. No one handles murder like you do."

"Donna," Mark protested. "Who didn't want me to take any cases? I think you told me not to answer the phone."

"That's before I knew it was Margery."

"Who isn't your close friend."

"That part is true, but I've known her for fifty years. We were in first grade together. I feel like I should do something."

"We're on our way to pick up Howard and Elizabeth."

"I know. I fixed the flags on the car and picked the music."

It didn't feel right to let a former classmate go unavenged. Not that Donna would dress in black and strap a sword to her back in her hunt for the murderer. Justice would be the best form of vengeance.

"You don't have to go full throttle. Just find out the facts and point out what they're not doing right."

"Ha! *That* would make me popular. You need to decide. I can work on the case or not."

If he did, it would leave her with sole hostess duties of the Scotland Yard Detective Inspector and his wife. She did have the supplies for a proper British tea ready.

"Well, knowing you and your great observation skills, you should have the case wrapped up in no time. Remember that the husband, Jeff, is a real dog. Makes passes at all the women in town."

Mark looked away from the road to his wife and growled, "Did he make a pass at you?"

Truthfully, she couldn't remember him doing so, which stung

her vanity, but he always preferred much younger females.

"*All* the women," she emphasized.

"Okay then, not you," he concluded with a nod.

No one could get anything past Detective Mark Taber. They pulled up in front of the police station, where Mark exited with a quick kiss. "This shouldn't take long. See you soon."

Donna took her place behind the wheel. While small talk wasn't her forte, she could locate two foreign tourists, drive them back to the inn, serve them tea, and tuck them up in their room. By that time, Mark should be back.

Chapter Two

THE HIGHWAY TRAFFIC picked up closer to the airport. Occasionally, a car would careen across the lanes, the driver realizing at the last minute they almost missed the exit to Charleston International Airport. There was a fairly good chance they were late, too.

Donna sniffed and muttered to herself. "Planning for various outcomes besides the desired one appears to be a skill not much in use."

The most recent wild-eyed driver with a car packed full of people might have wrongly assumed the traffic to be minimal. Not sure why, since Charleston served as an elegant tourist destination and possibly one of the most visited cities in the American South. While Donna enjoyed the historic city with its beautiful beaches, adorable boutiques, and exquisite restaurants, the airport sat in North Charleston, a more industrial area bordered by both the Air Force and Navy bases.

The airport itself, despite the *international* label, wasn't huge, and a good number of the planes taking off belonged to the Air Force adjoining airfield. There was no direct flight from London to Charleston, which meant poor Howard and Elizabeth stopped first in Dublin, then in Boston, hustled through customs, grabbed their luggage after inspection, and then boarded the plane to Charleston. Well, they should have if everything went as planned. There might have been a language barrier. Sure, they spoke the Queen's English, chock full of quaint expressions for everyday things, but customs agents might not understand them.

Her mouth twisted to one side as she flicked on her turn signal for the exit.

If they did run into *a spot of bother*—she grinned, realizing she'd just thought in British or possibly Winnie the Pooh—they'd call Mark. He would have called her if their positions were switched. She sighed. Did she suggest Mark dash off and solve the case? Oh, she knew she did but now realized she had failed to take into consideration her inability to recognize their guests. All she ever saw of the international travelers was a photo, and not a great one at that. Taken at an outdoor event, everyone sported hats. It didn't help they were surrounded by other proper British folks wearing hats, too.

Mark did point them out, but they hadn't much differed from the people around them. If she knew it would be an observational challenge, Donna would have searched for memorable marks, such as scars, a missing tooth, or even a birthmark shaped like a state. For all she knew, she may have stared at the wrong couple.

Nothing for it, she glared at the recreational vehicle big enough to house a Girl Scout troop in the lane she needed to be in. The driver neither let her ahead nor sped up enough for her to make a smooth transition behind. All she could see of the top of the driver's head remained fixed, never turning to peer at other cars.

Donna tapped the gas, shooting forward, but the RV driver must have seen it as a challenge and goosed his own pedal, also accelerating.

"Jerk!"

She allowed the lumbering behemoth to shoot ahead as she slowed and tucked herself behind it. There was no reason to take chances, especially not knowing the nature of the driver. It could be he'd had vehicles passing him right and left and decided he wasn't taking it anymore.

The light lilting sound of a flute from the CD player accompanied the sound of the tires on the road. So far, most of the songs depressed Donna. They centered on watching your true love sail away to be lost at sea, and loving someone who doesn't love you, but in your stupidity, you keep waiting. Maybe this next one might be a wee bit more cheerful. A clear tenor voice swelled out of the speakers.

"I'll do as much for my true love as any young man may. I'll sit and mourn all at her grave for a twelvemonth and a day."

Her mouth dropped open, and then she snapped it shut and turned off the music. "I can only hope our guests are more cheerful. The Beatles would be a lot more upbeat."

Rumor was they'd originally modeled themselves on girl bands like The Shirelles. Maybe she should ditch the music altogether.

Airport parking posed no problem. Donna hurried into the terminal, concerned with how she'd recognize the two. Travel magazines usually ran an article once a year on how not to look like an American when traveling. No-no's included wearing baseball hats, sportswear with college logos, athletic shoes, talking loudly, and smiling too much. The last one puzzled her. Should she glare at everyone if she traveled abroad?

The arrival and departures board showed the flight had arrived. Donna hurried to the open area where non-ticketed people could stand while waiting for travelers. Two TSA officials flanked the concourse exit and one had a German Shepherd on a short lead. Her lips drew down. Nothing says *Welcome!* like a fierce dog at the end of a leash.

Several flights must have arrived at once. A few families held up signs with the names of their loved ones. The first to come through the concourse were service members dressed in army fatigues and sporting wide grins. A few yips along with a polite smattering of applause sounded as children darted forward to embrace their parent. After that dramatic interlude, a parade of tired, rumpled people filed by, with many wearing baseball caps, a few sporting Gamecock shirts, even more with Crimson Tide shirts, and most wearing athletic shoes. For the most part, most weren't smiling with the exception of a young woman who glanced around expectantly to be met by her sweetheart carrying a sheath of roses.

Had she missed them? Donna turned slightly to watch the crowd hurry toward baggage. None of them fit the British profile of pale, uptight, quiet, and polite. Maybe they missed the plane. Dipping her hand into her purse to retrieve her phone, she caught sight of an older couple standing outside the restroom wearing straw fedoras. Not the expected head garb, but a hat, all the same. She hurried toward them, waving. "Howard and Elizabeth! Welcome."

A wide smile stretched across Donna's face as the female half of the couple shrank back and declared. "I think you have mistaken us for someone else."

Snowbird Yankee. She'd recognize the accent anywhere—East Coast with a touch of contempt. Money, but not so much that they had their own plane or hired their own jet. Donna's hand dropped along with her smile. Good manners dictated an appropriate response. "So sorry. Y'all have a nice day."

A tap on her left shoulder had her turning to face a middle-aged couple. The man had already lost a battle with a receding hairline. Catching Donna's gaze, he smiled, revealing an overlapping tooth. "I think you might be looking for us."

Both grinned at her as Donna schooled her face into something looking a bit less like shock. She found herself nodding her head as she surveyed their attire. Jeans. Sneakers. Who were they? Did they think she served as a driver? Maybe their driver failed to show on time and thought anyone standing about could be the missing chauffeur. Before Donna could formulate a response to clear up matters, she recognized the man's clipped manner of speaking. It was nothing elegant and cultured like the BBC shows, though.

"Howard? Elizabeth?"

"That's us," Elizabeth agreed with a nod.

"I'd thought you'd be wearing hats," Donna uttered the words, and then she realized how stupid they sounded.

"Wait," Elizabeth said and dug into her backpack. She pulled out a red cap with *Boston* stitched on the front. "I bought this at the last airport. Should I be wearing it?"

"No." The last thing the newly arrived Brits needed was to get the cold shoulder from the southerners who held a grudge almost two hundred years later over the War of Northern Aggression. "Let me show you to the baggage area. How did you recognize me?"

Howard puffed out his chest. "I am a Scotland Yard trained detective. Most of the people had already scattered, so not that many people to choose from. I then subtracted all the airport workers. Finally, I looked for a lush lady."

"Lush lady," she repeated the words, not liking the sound of them. Either they thought her a heavy drinker or overweight. Sure, she had to buy her clothing in the plus-size department, but only because the garment industry decided to end misses' sizes at twelve.

"Lush lady. That's how Mark described you."

Well, someone would be getting a chat tonight. Did he really think of her that way? He'd always assured her he loved her curves and not to change a thing. Was it just nonsense men say to keep their wives from chattering on?

A bewildered smile served as her response until she realized a verbal response might be expected. "Lovely."

Elizabeth sighed. "I can only hope my Howie talks about me in the same way."

Really? It had only taken five minutes for her to realize actual Brits were nothing like their television counterparts. "Okay. Let's go get your baggage."

She spoke as she herded her charges. "Did Mark let you know why he couldn't come to pick you up?"

"Yes." Howard waggled his brows. "Right chuffed about the idea of a murder. I'd love to see how Mark handles it." He placed a hand on his chest. "I'll be willing to lend a hand if he gets into a spot of trouble."

Trouble—that's what she had wrong before. It was trouble, not bother. As for helping, the commissioner would not be a fan. He never welcomed *her* insights, and she turned out to be right—most of the time.

Chapter Three

SUITCASES, USUALLY OF the plain black variety, chugged by on the groaning baggage belt. Every now and then a lime green or pink floral one made an appearance. Donna purchased purple luggage to avoid this issue, but the fact that more and more violet-hued suitcases had entered the travel world about the same time as her purchase didn't help. Focusing on the various colors of the baggage kept her from replaying the word *lush* the same way she worried an empty tooth socket with her tongue as a child.

It would be up to Mark to discourage Howard from offering a hand. By the time they arrived, the husband, Jeff, could already be in custody. The metal clicks of the conveyor belt registered as Donna considered her deceased schoolmate, Margery. There was nothing unusual about her. She'd given Donna a run as far as setting the biology grade curve. Not too surprisingly, as a bookish female who seldom raised her voice, she served as the town librarian for almost a quarter of a century. Her conservative clothing and thick glasses solidified the librarian image. There was nothing surprising about Margery except for Jeff, her handsome, player husband. He came along later when the librarian hit forty and inherited her family's estate on the edge of Legacy.

The flash of the Union Jack in the form of a hard-sided suitcase had Donna moving forward since Howard and Elizabeth stood as still as rabbits hoping not to be detected by a nearby dog. Obviously, they didn't know you had to wade in and grab your luggage. It made her wonder how they managed to get through customs in Boston.

She muttered, "Excuse me," as she made her way to the rapidly vanishing suitcase. Her hand shot out and snared the colorful bag before it made another trip around.

Donna hefted the heavy case to the ground and glanced back at Howard and Elizabeth, who shook their heads. As far as she knew, a head shake also meant no in Britain. Their twin surprised expressions didn't register gratitude, that much she could see. Then an elderly Asian lady tapped Donna on the arm.

"Thanks for getting my bag. Can you put it on my cart now?"

Donna pulled the cumbersome bag in question behind her, then hefted it onto a stainless-steel cart travelers rented if they had a multitude of bags. When she glanced back to her guests, they both had medium-sized, non-descript bags by their side. Her cheeks flushed, she hurried back to her guests before someone else asked for help with their luggage.

"Sorry. I thought the bag was yours."

Elizabeth chuckled and nudged her husband. "See, I told you." She wrinkled her nose and added, "Howard would never allow me to buy such a garish bag. Too obvious."

"It would make it easy to pick out on a belt," Donna pointed out. While a suitcase worked to contain clothes and other necessities, it failed if someone picked up yours for theirs, which happened more than people might suspect.

"Easy for thieves, too," Howard added.

He inhaled, folded his hands behind his back, and then shot Donna a look—the same type she might use on Jasper when he piddled on the floor. Most of the doctors at her old hospital job occasionally managed a similar expression while schooling the nurses on an issue they already knew.

"Thieves could take *any* bag," she felt compelled to mention. "They're not shopping for fashion, but contents. More likely, they'd be familiar with the top designer brands and go for a Louis Vuitton or a Gucci bag."

One eyebrow lifted as Howard announced, "Aces."

That sounded slightly better than *lush*, that much she knew. Even though her guests would only be here a week, she didn't want them to think she was either the stupid or the greedy American stereotype that showed up in police dramas. She'd thought she made her point as she gestured for them to follow her to the car, but Howard cleared his throat, which was always Mark's thing for getting attention. What did the man have to say now?

"The eye-catching luggage you hefted off the belt shouts foreign tourist."

Foreign tourist? You'd think they'd have a bunch of those cases arriving in the London airport. Maybe he meant seeing it in the US. If so, she could have told him it's easy enough to get one online, and there were plenty of Anglophiles, even in South Carolina. Not wanting to cause any trouble for the long ride home, she kept her mouth shut, mostly. "Why would this be a bad thing?"

"Good question," Howard commented before launching into his next mini-lecture as they strolled through the car garage. "Foreign travel isn't cheap."

Even as a non-world traveler, Donna knew this.

Elizabeth moved closer and whispered, "So good of you to humor him. He needs a new audience now and then to expound his various theories."

"They're *facts*," Howard assured with certainty in his voice. "It's been proven. London is one of the busiest airports in the world.

Because of that, it can be a hotbed of crime for the unwary tourist."

"How so?" Donna found herself intrigued, even if Howard managed a bit of a know-it-all air. When it came to crime in big airports, maybe he did know it all.

"Well, back to the foreign traveler. A thief realizes the traveler must have money to go abroad. It makes sense they'd have some nice clothes and even jewelry or electronics tucked away in their bag."

Electronics? "Have you seen how they handle the bags? I lost a front pocket on my weekender suitcase on a simple trip to South Florida."

"Not all people are as savvy as you about airlines. Still, it is simple for the well-dressed thief to snag a bag and be on his way, only to return later with a slight costume change for another bag."

"What about…" Donna intended to ask about the baggage claim stubs the airlines issue to prove a bag belongs to you but realized she never had to prove a bag was her own. Not much security there, but she had switched to TSA-approved locks on her suitcases to prevent random pawing of her underthings in search of the family pearls. Realizing she'd left her question hanging and had Howard and Elizabeth waiting for her to finish, she changed the content. "Airport employees. A few have been caught stealing thousands of dollars of travelers' goods."

"Sadly, yes." Howard agreed, and his voice dropped a bit, before swinging up again. "In London, we have everything on CC television. If there's a problem, we can go back and look at the film and find the culprit. Of course, at an international airport, we need to be notified immediately before the culprit boards a plane and vanishes."

Closed-circuit television had come up in more than one of her favorite British mysteries. The criminals definitely knew about it, often staying out of range or having their faces shadowed by hats, hoodies, or sunglasses so as not to be identified. All in all, they still must be a huge help in solving crimes.

Donna pointed her fob at her sedan and pressed it to unlock. "Anything else I should worry about if I'm in the London airport?"

"Aye." Howard gave a muffled chuckle, lifted his suitcase into the open trunk, and then did the same with his wife's. "There's the fake porters who help you with your luggage as you blithely dash off to your plane. Pickpockets infest the airport. You never know your documents or wallet have been lifted until you need them. Don't forget about the RFID lifters."

RFID? The acronym sounded familiar, but she couldn't quite place it. Taking her silence for ignorance, Howard hurried to explain. "Radio Frequency Identification. Most credit cards and bank cards have one now. It allows you to wave your card at the local tea shop without even inserting it into the machine. This convenience makes it equally easy for those with a listening device to get close enough to you to pull your number and information for their own use."

"Oh, that." Donna remembered the issue and had even bought a special wallet to deal with it. "I've taken care of that. I have a special wallet to block the signals."

Howard slammed the trunk closed and gave Donna an approving smile. "Smart. Did you know wallets and sleeves advertised to safeguard your number don't always work? I can give you a number of examples."

Donna sighed. It would be a long trip back to Legacy.

Chapter Four

SUNLIGHT SLID INTO the airport parking garage as Donna circled the car. A wave of her hand indicated the unlocked doors. Donna forced a smile, waiting to see who would sit where. When people rode together, dating couples might sit together, while long-married ones separated to catch up with their friends during the ride. This division depended on having four people though. Whoever chose the passenger seat would be her conversational partner for the ride home.

So far, Howard proved to be the chatty one, and she suspected his topic of conversation would possibly be all of his exploits. Truthfully, she wouldn't mind hearing one or two of his tales. When would she have another chance to talk to an actual Scotland Yard Detective Inspector? She might pick up some new sleuthing angles.

Still, the three-plus hours home might be a bit more than she could stomach. Elizabeth might be the shyer of the two, or it could be she never had a chance to get a word in edgewise. When Howard held the passenger front door wide for his wife, Donna released her held breath. All should be well. If nothing else, she could always resort to the British folk songs CD. Perhaps they'd like it more than she did.

Her guests remained quiet, checking their cell phones and possibly assuring friends and family on the other side of the pond that they'd made it. This interlude provided enough time to work her way out of the garage, pay the attendant, and merge onto I-26 heading home.

After passing a few billboards, one with a three-dimensional sausage attached to it and lettering that declared you never *sausage* a place, Elizabeth asked, "What is South of the Line, and are we stopping there?"

Biscuits and gravy. Of all the signs she had to fixate on, she had picked that one. Not exactly the image she wanted for her part of the country. "It's not much, really. I think it may have started as a motor lodge."

"A what?" Elizabeth inquired.

"It's a cheap place to stay where people park their car outside their door. Just the basics." Donna hoped to discourage any interest in the place with its cartoon mascot with an oversized sombrero screaming word puns. No way would Elizabeth know the phrase *South of the Line* normally referred to Mexico, and most everything within the walls of the inaccurately named tourist trap were ancient stereotypes of their neighbor to the south, including the giant sombrero tower.

Another colorful sign, which Donna sincerely hoped her passenger had missed, showed a large open-mouthed gator.

"Look, Howard. It's an alligator. I didn't think we'd have an opportunity to see one in its natural habitat," Elizabeth announced and then let out a squeal worthy of any pre-teen girl at a boy band concert. "I can't wait to tell my friends back home."

"It's far from its natural habitat," Donna felt compelled to say.

"Probably so," Howard agreed, sitting way too close for him to be successfully seat belted in place. "Still, it might be fun."

Images of a semi cutting them off, resulting in slammed brakes and one of London's Finest hitting the windshield filled Donna's mind. Requesting a grown man and an officer of the law to use his seatbelt would probably have little to no effect. As she fought to rein in her imagination from feeding her dire scenarios, she grumbled, "Tourist trap."

"I suspect it is," Howard replied from his perch right behind Donna's shoulders. "People flock to London to see Big Ben or The London Eye. They're tourist traps, too."

"Better ones, for sure, but I can see your point." She gave a little chuckle, remembering when she was a child begging to stop to see the sights of South of the Line. There had to be a lot fewer sights back then, too.

In her memory, her father chose to stop, buying her a multi-colored serape, and snapped her picture near a concrete burro while she savored an ice cream cone. "Well, I will warn you. There's a huge gift shop, restaurants, a gas station, and, of course, the motor lodge."

"Don't forget the alligators," Elizabeth reminded her with enthusiasm.

Yep, they were definitely going to stop. "Despite the number of billboards, it's probably a good ninety minutes away." Donna pressed her lips together, trying to consider how she might get Howard to sit back in his seat and buckle up.

"Does it feel like I'm going faster than you usually travel in London?" If he could read through the lines, he'd buckle up.

"Oh, aye, bloody fast." He coughed and then cleared his throat. "London traffic slows any commute to a crawl. An officer on foot can sometimes reach a crime scene faster than I can."

Good heavens, the man had a dry throat. Not unusual for flying and she hustled them into a car for the long ride home without a thought to their comfort. What a terrible hostess. Donna watched the road information signs for the next possibility of a drink. Ideally, she'd love a place with a wraparound veranda and big hanging ferns and maybe a cordial hostess bedecked in a ruffly apron who'd call them *honey* and fuss over them. A billboard sign with *Auntie Ethel's Diner* on it had her clicking on the turn signal and hoping Ethel embodied the charm most genteel Southern women possessed.

"We're going to make a brief sweet tea stop."

"Oh, good," Elizabeth enthused. "A nice cuppa would be lovely."

British television taught that a *cuppa* equaled hot tea. No one would want hot tea with the temps soaring past ninety degrees.

"You'll love it," Donna promised. Very few people didn't fall under the spell of sweet tea.

Happy about the possibility that a tiny part of her welcoming mission would pass muster, she followed the pointing arrows directing her to Auntie Ethel. No gracious rambling building with a wraparound porch existed on either side of the road. "I'm looking for Auntie Ethel's and a cold, tall glass of delicious, iced tea."

"You been there before?" Howard prompted, still practically breathing on her neck. Did they not have personal boundaries in Britain?

"No." She pushed out the word while projecting a mental image of the man safely buckled in his seat. Not for the first time, she wished Mark had accompanied her. This would be much easier if her role consisted of providing historical facts about the area as opposed to being chauffeur, tour guide, and reluctant safety monitor.

"Would it be that orange place to your left?" Elizabeth offered, gesturing to a small, shabby building with faded orange paint.

It had the look of a fast-food restaurant—one that had seen hard times. A faded sign identified it as their destination. A couple of pickup trucks in the lot testified to its openness, which ruined any possibility of bypassing it with a murmured excuse of it being closed.

"Ah, yes." Missing the place and then complaining about it being too hard to make the turn in traffic crossed her mind, except the lack of traffic would prevent the excuse from flying. Howard coughed hard—in her ear. Only a mean person would ignore his dry throat. The questionable restaurant would have something cold inside, hopefully in a clean, disposable cup. Donna signaled and made a neat turn into the lot. "I'll just run in and grab us some…"

Before she could finish, Howard and Elizabeth had opened their doors and exited. She did, likewise, knowing she'd not be able to stuff them back into the car against their wills.

Elizabeth sidled closer to her and asked in a loud whisper.

"Do you think they have a loo?"

State law required restrooms for employees and possibly customers, but the bigger question centered on the cleanliness of the facilities. "Ah, I'll have to check it out," Which meant wipe down everything with the bleach wipes she kept in her purse for situations such as this. "Most likely."

"That would be tickety boo."

Donna pursed her lips, clueless to what Elizabeth meant. There was a good chance she needed to clean up the women's restroom super-fast. Howard, on the other hand, was on his own. Being a Scotland Yard Detective Inspector came with a certain amount of risk.

Might as well get a move on, or they'd be even later than she anticipated. If this humble place satisfied their drink and bathroom needs, they might be able to resist the lure of South of the Line. A wave of frosty air escaped as she pushed the door open. The air conditioning worked, which was a plus. Her eyes traveled over the aged booths with clean Formica topped tables. A couple of men dawdled over an impressive stack of pancakes with syrup running over the side.

A heavy-set woman with unnaturally black hair garbed in a cook's apron turned at their entrance and gave them an energetic wave, followed by, "Howdy!"

Donna stiffened in spite of the woman's friendliness. A cut of her eyes showed her guests hadn't detected the hard northern accent of a Northern transplant trying to make a go of it. She couldn't blame them for wanting to escape the harsh winters, but what could Ethel know of Southern cooking?

The woman must have mistaken Donna's full stop for uncertainty. "Sit anywhere," she said and gestured to the several empty booths.

Howard, not needing to be told twice, promptly took a nearby booth while Elizabeth shifted her weight foot-to-foot, glancing around the place.

Without being told of her need, the cook pointed to the right, sending Elizabeth hotfooting it to the facilities. As the guide, chaperone, and bathroom inspector, Donna dashed to get in front of Elizabeth and inside the restroom first.

She slammed the door on an open-mouthed Elizabeth before surveying the single-person toilet. No trash on the floor, no graffiti on the walls, and a clean scent of pine hung in the air. Not bad at all. Donna turned to leave but made a point to wash her hands. When she opened the door, she gave Elizabeth a sheepish grin.

"Former nurse. I'm all about washing my hands. Call me germ-phobic."

Instead of replying, Elizabeth darted inside and locked the door. Might as well see what Howard might be up to in her absence.

A huge slab of apple pie with butter melting on top rested beside a steaming cup of coffee. Howard picked up his fork with a wide grin. "I had to try the apple pie to see if it matches up to our own apple crumble."

The flaky golden crust embraced firm, juicy apples that had Donna holding her hand up to catch the server's attention. A small piece wouldn't hurt. Call it professional curiosity. The woman she assumed to be Ethel came bustling toward them, carrying two sweating glasses with red plastic straws sticking out. She placed them on the table with a grin. "I thought you ladies might like a refreshing beverage. This is my mint tea."

Donna had the glass halfway to her mouth as she processed the words. Mint tea as opposed to sweet tea. She took a cautious sip, allowing the crisp liquid to slide down her throat. Then she took another, just to be sure. It certainly tasted nothing like the sugar syrup that normally passed for sweet tea. All the same, she liked it. "This is good."

Ethel gave a hearty belly laugh that caused her apron to bounce up and down. "It always pleases me to hear a Southerner admit that a Yankee can make decent tea."

By that time, Elizabeth strolled up during the last bit of the sentence and gave Donna an astounded look. "Isn't everyone here a Yank?"

Chapter Five

A FAMILIAR SILHOUETTE of a man backlit by the porch lights greeted Donna as she made the turn into The Painted Lady Inn parking lot. Despite the long summer light, the clouds turned a reddish violet with the sky heading toward indigo. Snores filled the sedan as Donna carefully parked the car and slid down the window.

Mark abandoned his watch and trotted down the stairs to greet her. "What happened?"

Donna placed a finger to her lips. "Shush! They're finally asleep. I hate to wake them." She turned to look at Elizabeth, who cuddled a stuffed alligator. Even though South of the Line was not on her itinerary, the place managed to get Howard to buckle up with a sign that reminded *y'all to buckle up and come back.*

"They wanted to stop at every kitschy roadside attraction. Let's say billboards were not wasted on them. Howard just dozed off in the middle of a story about a woman who impersonated the queen. Quite frankly, I want to know how it ends."

Mark chuckled softly, "I bet you can get him to finish it. Let's get them to bed."

The two of them worked in tandem with Mark carrying the luggage and Donna herding the drowsy guests like a sheepdog. Instead of the pen, she led them into the elevator and eventually to their room. A quick instruction on the breakfast procedure probably meant nothing to the bleary-eyed couple, who could wake up in the middle of the night expecting a snack only to find everyone tucked in bed. If nothing else, the snack nooks on every level would serve.

Making sure to keep her footsteps quiet, Donna crept down the stairs. The sound of a television playing behind one of the doors reminded her that they had other guests. Thank goodness her mother and Maria stood in for her as she made the airport run. Tomorrow will be more ordinary. She crossed her fingers just to be sure.

At the bottom of the steps, Mark met her. "Hungry?"

Her hand spread over her belly and as she moaned. "Not for food. I had the tamale pie. Right now, I might need an antacid."

"Poor baby," Mark cooed and wrapped an arm around her shoulders. "How about I make you a cup of peppermint tea."

"Sounds good." Donna leaned against her husband, glad to be home. "You know what would be even better?" she purred in a flirtatious fashion.

"Mmmm, I bet I can guess. However, I also bet you'd like the rundown on what I found out today."

"Ah." She gave his hand a playful tap. "You know me so well."

"That I do, which explains why I'm such a great detective." He guided her into the kitchen where Donna took a seat on a stool by the work island and watched as her husband made tea.

"Husband guilty, right?"

"Possibly." Mark gave a non-committal answer as he pulled a cup from the cabinet. He filled it with water and then put it in the microwave before elaborating. "Turns out the husband wasn't even home. He was in NYC for a dental convention. He took his cute little hygienist along with him, which means he wasn't in the area."

Unwilling to give up her first suspicion as the husband being the guilty party, Donna held up one finger. "He could have *said* he was in New York and be down the street taking the call."

"He could have, but I talked to his secretary, who had no reason to lie since she didn't know anything about the wife being dead until I told her."

Even though the population of Legacy had grown by almost a hundred residents last year, it still kept its small-town feel, including the gossip hotline. "I knew about the murder before I left this morning. Why wouldn't the secretary know?"

"As far as I know, she isn't married to anyone on the force. Believe it or not, just because you know something doesn't mean everyone else does. With that in mind, keep this under your hat."

He made it sound like she'd go blabbing. *Please*. She stuck out her tongue, which resulted in Mark chuckling. The microwave beeped. Her husband finished making her tea and delivered it to her with a grin.

"I know you won't. I'm not worried about you, but I am about Cecilia. You know she's tied into the town's gossip network."

"So true. Mother has her finger on the town's pulse." She picked up the hot cup of tea and blew on it before taking a sip. "Good tea."

"Ha! I'm the champ at throwing a tea bag into a cup." He pulled up a stool and joined her. "I know you want to know what I know or suspect."

"You bet."

He spread his hand on the island. "You know the drill."

Donna took another sip of her tea, not answering, waiting to get a reaction. Mark waited wordlessly, showing neither impatience nor frustration. His ability to keep a straight face served him well during questioning. While some big-city cops worked the good cop / bad cop angle, Mark settled for being more neutral than anything else.

Jasper's raspy snores served as the only sound if she discounted the low hum of the fridge. Wait. The older dog hadn't even come out to greet her. She stretched out her leg with the intention of nudging her old puggle but stopped short of doing it. The years were catching up with her trusted canine.

Instead, she grinned at her husband. "Yeah, I know the drill. I'll tell you what I know and find out what I don't."

Chapter Six

Donna turned in bed and pounded her pillow. Whenever she went to bed late, sleep eluded her. She ended up watching the red numerals on her bedside clock instead. Most of the night would be spent counting the hours of slumber she might manage if she immediately closed her eyes and caught some Zs.

Raspy snores filled the bedroom. Jasper, who slept in his dog bed, often lapsed into noisy sleep sometimes punctuated with whimpering that indicated being chased by bigger dogs or a delicious bone just out of reach. The canine ruckus bypassed Mark. He entered dreamland when his head hit the pillow. A great skill for a cop who often had limited opportunities for rest.

A cabinet door slammed closed in the distance. In a full inn, occasional sounds happened. Usually, a creak of overhead steps or a flush of the toilet signaled a restless guest. A cabinet slam meant someone making free with her kitchen. As a bed and breakfast owner, she soon discovered a few guests mistook the inn for their own home, which resulted in her padlocking the basement, which she used for storage, the liquor cabinet, and her sub-zero fridge. At best, her sleepless guests could make coffee or help themselves to snacks. A metallic clang had her sitting upright. Were they cooking *and* trashing her kitchen?

Donna sighed hard and then glanced at her husband to see if the sound woke him. It hadn't. There was no choice but to handle it herself. She sat up in bed and reached for her robe draped at the foot of her bed for such an event. She shrugged on the robe, grumbling and hoping to stir at least one of the males to accompany her on the mission. No luck.

Just before she cracked the door, the thought of a burglar crossed her mind. It would be either an extremely bold or a stupid move to rob an inn full of people. Still, it wouldn't be the first time. Her hand landed on the object nearest the door, an old-fashioned metal bed warmer she'd recently picked up at a swap meet. Her fingers tightened around the handle as she swung the door open.

Her bare feet padded toward the sound of indecipherable conversation and muffled feminine laughter. Hardened criminals seldom giggled, or at least they didn't in police dramas. Her shoulders relaxed as she put her hand on the swing-thru kitchen door.

"Oh, hello!" Donna pretended surprise at seeing a bare-chested young man in pajama pants lounging against the counter and a woman dressed in an oversized T-shirt in the process of popping a strawberry into her mouth. Obviously, Donna hadn't locked the fridge. She placed the unneeded bedwarmer beside the door. It didn't look like she'd be braining anyone with it.

The woman waved to the fridge. "Join us. There's lots of goodies inside."

Donna arched her eyebrows. "I know. I happen to be the owner of the inn. Some of those goodies are intended for breakfast tomorrow."

That caused the man to change his casual stance to an upright one. He cleared his throat. "Sorry about that. We didn't know the owner slept on the premises. Didn't mean to disturb you."

The woman placed the half-eaten strawberry back into the bowl, contaminating all the other berries. The germophobe inside Donna winced, resulting in her pushing the bowl toward them. "Take those. There's a snack nook on each floor you can visit. It's full of snacks and drinks."

"I know." The woman replied and wrinkled her nose. "But I wanted something fresh."

Irritation settled on her shoulders initially at the mention of not knowing the owners were on the premises. The unspoken message meant they expected to make free with everything within the inn. It made her wonder if this was their normal practice. Then the female partner implied her snacks were old. The remark chafed. "Well, you have something fresh now to take up to your room."

A door creaked in the back hall before a sleepy Thelma, the live-in assistant, wandered into the kitchen, blinking. "I felt a disturbance in the atmosphere."

The female guest who respected no boundaries addressed Donna, "Does she always talk like that?"

"Pretty much." Even though Thelma had only been working at the inn a few months, Donna had become used to her sometime psychic helper, who talked like a character from a fantasy novel. To be fair, sometimes her predictions proved true.

Almost on cue, Thelma held her hands up as if surrendering or calling down lightning. "Danger is awakening."

Unfortunately for Margery, the warning came a little late, but it served to get the kitchen raiders moving and up to their room. Both Thelma and Donna stared at the still swinging door. "Thanks for your bogus prediction. It worked. We may have to keep our eyes on those two and their night roaming ways."

"We definitely should keep our eyes on them." Thelma gave a sage nod before speaking in a somber tone. "They aren't the real danger. Trouble is unfolding like a flower, a deadly one."

Donna closed her eyes briefly, thinking now it's going to be really hard to sleep with such a pronouncement. Her eyes snapped open when she remembered the unlocked fridge. "I'll lock the fridge. Right about now, I'd like to bar the kitchen door. We'd better get to bed since morning comes fast."

★

HER WORDS PROVED true as Donna slept through her alarm and had to be nudged awake by her husband.

"Honey, you might want to get up and get the coffee started before the guests start moaning about a caffeine deficit."

Donna grumbled under her breath and burrowed into the pillow. "Maybe they'll sleep late since they were wandering around after midnight."

"That's only some of them. Tell you what. I'll get up and start breakfast."

The kind suggestion woke Donna up in no time. Her half-opened eyes stared at the bedside table and the arm of her husband. Mark might grill a mean burger, but that summed up his cooking ability.

"Okay, I'm up. Maybe you should check on our folks across the pond. I would have expected them to be in my kitchen, but not the young couple I caught red-handed raiding the fridge."

It only took her few minutes to dress. Jasper joined Donna as she made her way to the kitchen. Fortunately, Thelma had turned on the oven and scurried around the kitchen filling up glass bottles filled with various juices and milk.

"Coffee?" Donna inquired hopefully.

"It's already perking in the oversized urn in the dining room,"

Thelma answered with a knowing smirk. "I usually do that first. Surprised you slept late."

"Me, too," Donna said, "I'm just grateful you were up and moving. We have a full inn and those guests from England. I know they'll want their tea. We need to have their hot water and a pitcher full of cream ready pronto. I'm surprised they haven't been downstairs in search of a good cuppa."

Voices on the stairs had Donna dashing to fill the tea thermos with hot water while Thelma placed a cream pitcher and a plate of biscotti on the small table used for tea service. A couple of white stoneware cups with saucers crowded next to the thermos.

The clipped tones of her foreign guests wafted down the stairs along with her husband's baritone. Mark would guide them to the tea station. Donna slipped into the kitchen but stayed just inside the door to hear the reception her stocked tea stand would get, especially since she'd stopped by Pam's Tea World to pick up Prince of Wales and English Breakfast teabags.

"Here's your morning tea," Mark announced.

"What's that?" Howard asked with his British accent that conveyed the impression that he'd stepped in something offensive. "Skinny toast?"

"Biscotti. Twice-baked flavored biscuits usually served with coffee."

It was a fair answer, Donna would give her husband that, as she pressed her ear against the door to hear more. No raptures about her having British tea, only something indistinguishable with Mark saying, "We'll see."

She barely had a chance to get her cheek off the door as her husband pushed on it, only to be stopped by her body. Thankfully, he barely pushed it as if suspecting she might be on the other side.

Donna slid back a step and raised an inquisitive brow.

"They need milk with their tea. Would you possibly have PG Tips or Barry's Tea?"

Seriously? One hand found purchase on her hip. "If they wanted special orders, they needed to tell me in advance. It's printed on the website. No, I do not have whatever they asked for. I assumed they'd like Prince of Wales or English Breakfast—after all, they have to do with England."

"I know you've worked hard to make things nice. I think a simple, strong, black tea would serve."

Donna moved toward the cabinet where she kept the teabags as she speculated on how much trouble her foreign visitors might be. She pulled out a carton of the local supermarket tea. "Tell Elizabeth it's American. It's my understanding she wants to experience American culture."

"Will do," Mark answered, "Oh, Howard saw you had scones on the breakfast menu. He wanted to know if you had clotted cream and lemon curd."

Having hosted numerous high teas at the inn, this one she knew and had planned for. "Tell him, yes we do, along with some delicious local jams."

Her husband winked before stepping out of the kitchen.

Bottles clanged as Thelma lifted the tray of juices to carry into the dining room. Before she left the kitchen, she angled her head to the hall. "Those foreigners. They've got something to do with the danger. Not sure if they brought it with them or if it's coming *for* them."

On that note, she left. Like so many of her other statements, it remained a bit ambiguous. If Thelma were a meteorologist, she'd probably say it would rain or not.

Chapter Seven

THE REQUEST FOR milk as opposed to cream for her British guests' tea had Donna biting her lip as opposed to slapping her forehead. She knew about the milk, but lack of sleep and waking up late resulted in her not thinking everything through. While most people could shrug things off, Donna's desire to be right made it difficult to go with the flow. Breakfast would make up for her dairy fumble.

She moved back to the hot stove to fry wide, thick-cut bacon strips to crispy goodness even though her idea of an English breakfast came from a restaurant menu she'd found online. The tropical restaurant listed various breakfasts including European, which consisted of a hard roll and fruit while the American version offered bacon, eggs, and a choice of toast. The British selection included baked beans, sliced tomatoes, English muffin, linked sausage, bacon, and eggs, along with a pot of tea. It might be more of a weekend spread as opposed to a weekday meal. Still, it would be a treat for her across-the-pond guests.

The door creaked as Thelma hurried back in with her empty tray. "The natives are getting restless. Are the pastries ready? I heard someone ask for a donut."

Donna shivered at the prospect. "Donuts." She donned a heat-resistant mitt and opened the oven, releasing scented warm air heavy with blueberry, orange, and caramel aromas. "Get these out," she directed and placed the warm pastries on the island. "The muffins should be ready soon."

"Got it," Thelma acknowledged as she reached for the baskets normally used for bread. As she transferred the pastries to the cloth napkin-lined basket, she pushed a can of baked beans out of the way. "What's with the beans?"

"British thing." Donna shrugged. "Heard they like beans and toast." She made a mental note to herself to start the toast.

Instead of answering with a cryptic comment, as usual, Thelma moved the filled baskets to the tray and ferried them to the dining room. An increase in conversation levels on the other side of the door meant either more guests had arrived or verbal appreciation of the still warm pastries.

Fresh fruit came next. Thankfully, the citrus heavy fruit salad had been made ahead, which meant it only had to be dished out. Early on in her B and B visions, she'd planned to serve her guests with plated entrées, but soon discovered it would take much more help than she had to do so. Instead, they employed what she jokingly referred to as a *segmented buffet* since not everything came out at the same time. A handwritten menu told guests what to expect to make sure they didn't leave before the main entrée arrived.

The door complained as Thelma hurried back and forth carrying all the items from the menu for the regular guests, including a frittata that just finished warming. Donna dashed about the kitchen arranging her proper British breakfast. She slid the sunny side up eggs onto the plate next to the baked beans, link sausage, toast, and a buttered English muffin. Normally, Thelma and sometimes Mark helped deliver the entrées. Her husband's absence meant he must be keeping Howard and Elizabeth company.

Once she arranged everything to her specifications, she hefted the heavy tray with pride, thinking it looked even better than the image featured on the restaurant's website. "They're going to love this."

Donna carefully backed out of the kitchen before turning to the dining room. Used dishes littered a few of the round tables, which had Thelma alternating between topping off beverages and clearing tables. Near the window that overlooked the flower garden, Mark's broad back blocked her ability to see Elizabeth and Howard well. She assumed the hair, legs, and arms of the seated couple belonged to the Brits.

A few of the seated guests called out, curious about the destination of the humongous breakfast. Donna had been perfecting her image of the genial innkeeper. So far, she still had to excuse herself when she felt the need to school someone. Saying, "Not you!" might sound abrupt. Instead, Donna responded with a big smile and a hearty, "Beautiful morning."

Her long strides carried her to the table in question. Several small, empty plates crowded the surface along with half-empty glasses and teacups. Donna stopped abruptly, her eyes widening as the situation sunk in. They had already eaten. She shot an accusatory glance at her husband, who shrugged.

Elizabeth, spotting her, waved. "Good morning."

"Morning," Donna offered, her arms aching, holding the heavy tray steady. Would the two still be hungry? From the empty dishes, they must have tied on the feedbag with a vengeance.

Elizabeth half stood to see the contents of Donna's tray. "That looks good. What is it?"

The woman's innocent inquiry caused Donna to swallow hard. Surely a Brit would recognize a full English breakfast. "What do you usually have for breakfast?"

"Tea and toast," Howard said with an accompanying head shake. "Some days I don't even get that."

"Nothing like this sumptuous spread." Elizabeth patted her stomach. "I'm stuffed. I can't eat another thing."

"Me, either." Howard echoed the sentiment. "Just as well, I need to get moving. Mark is going to show me how American constables solve a crime."

The announcement astounded her, especially since the commissioner discouraged Donna from helping. Perhaps Howard misunderstood. Why would the fussy commissioner allow a foreigner to stick his nose where it didn't belong? Screaming muscles and a streak of peevishness wide enough to drive a semi through had Donna whirling with her tray, causing the plates to clang.

For a few loaded seconds, the proper British breakfast slid precariously as Donna sucked in her breath and managed to balance it. Once settled, she decided not to waste her hard work and returned to her curious diners and offered them a full British breakfast. One of the diners gifted with a second breakfast requested hot sauce, which meant a return trip to the kitchen.

Just as well, she slammed her empty tray on the island, earning a judgmental glance from her dog, who she'd awakened. "Sorry, Jasper."

Dogs excelled at creating guilt in their humans. Her hand went to her neck, rubbing out the tension. How would Howard and Elizabeth know they had a special meal in store when her husband didn't know? Her momentary upset floated away as she tidied the area. The swinging door creaked open, and Donna remembered the hot sauce.

"Just a minute." She opened a cabinet and pulled out two different bottles of sauce. One promised a spicy time, and the other had a guy's hat blowing off from the heat. "Here ya go." She turned expecting Thelma but met Mark's questioning stare.

Thelma popped in behind him and leaned around the detective to grab the bottles from Donna. "I'd better hurry. The man is going through the food like a hot knife through butter."

Mark cleared this throat after the door swung close. "You're upset. I didn't know you were going to make a special breakfast for them."

"Forget about that." She picked up a damp cloth and wiped down the island, herding all the crumbs to her cupped hand. What he didn't mention was the fact Howard got to work on a Legacy murder investigation.

"Hmm," Mark murmured and reached for Donna's arm, but she danced out of the way while continuing to clean. He sighed. "It's obvious you're still upset. They loved the food. Elizabeth is all about experiencing everything American. That should make you happy."

Donna spun, placing her hands behind her on the island and arched her eyebrows at her husband. "Food? You think I'm mad about food?"

"You're not?" He shook his head as if the possibility surprised him. His brow furrowed as he contemplated the situation. Just when Donna opened her mouth, he held up a finger. "I got it. You're mad I'm taking Howard to work with me to help."

He folded his arms and managed a pleased expression. "I was going to take Howard to work with me before the murder. Everyone wants to meet him, including the commissioner. He's like a rock star. He works for Scotland Yard. It would be the equivalent of you meeting Julia Child or Alice Waters or some of those other famous chefs."

As much as it pained her to admit it, he had a point. Donna pushed off the island and put away the open food items. "Julia Child has transitioned to the great kitchen, so I won't see her soon. I'm not sure why everyone considers a Scotland Yard Detective Inspector so much better than you."

What she didn't say was why did Howard get so much better treatment than she received when assisting with a case?

"Not better," Mark clarified. "I assume the Brits have different ways of looking at things. Who knows? He might offer some helpful tips that will allow us to solve the murder faster."

Donna watched all the BBC crime dramas, which should make her just about as valuable as Howard, but no one ever asked for her advice besides Mark. "They've only asked him because he's a man."

"*And* a veteran Scotland Yard Detective Inspector. He's closed dozens of cases."

Well, they both knew she couldn't claim dozens of cases to her name. Donna folded her arms as her lips folded into a mulish expression.

Her husband assumed the discussion finished, gave her a quick kiss and then added, "You got Elizabeth. Go do something American. She'll love it."

Chapter Eight

"**D**O SOMETHING AMERICAN." Donna repeated the words to herself after her husband exited the kitchen, leaving the door swinging in his wake. The little women stayed safe getting their nails done and stopping for afternoon tea at A Little Bit of Paris Café. Okay, her cuticles could benefit from some attention, and snacking on someone else's baking could count as research.

Caught up in possible plans for the day, Donna stood motionless in the middle of the kitchen clutching a damp dishtowel in one wet hand and an oversized bowl in the other. The kitchen door eased open as Thelma backed in, carrying a tray stacked high with dirty dishes. She took a few quick steps and placed the unwieldy tray on the island with a hard thump, which caused the stacked dishes to cascade. Both Donna and Thelma leaped into action to catch the dishes before they reached the hard floor.

A tinkling of silverware and the crystalline shatter of a couple of juice glasses set Jasper barking, possibly startled from his morning snooze.

"Whoa!" An unfamiliar voice came from beyond the door. "What's going on in there?"

Thelma straightened from her crouched position and half-turned toward the door, but Donna shook her head, discouraging her assistant from answering the question. A few things Donna learned from trial and error was guests often said things that didn't need to be addressed.

A few hadn't appreciated Donna's effort to be as historically accurate as possible with some of the décor and asked if her dead grandmother had decorated the place. In that situation, she went to her tried and true method of dealing with rude guests, which was to ignore them. Her second tool in her genial innkeeper bag of tricks involved saying random remarks having nothing to do with the original query. This confused most, even to the point of forgetting about their original question.

She held out her hand with her palm flat like a policeman halting traffic. Thelma kept her lips sealed until the voices grew smaller and finally ended with the front door shutting. A heavy exhale sounded, followed by Thelma wincing.

"Sorry about the dishes."

"No problem," Donna acknowledged as she moved toward the closet that contained the broom and dustpan. "Why don't you keep Jasper in place, and I'll sweep up."

After the broken glass vanished into the trash can, Thelma glanced up from her position beside Jasper, who wiggled in delight at the belly rubs he'd received. "You're still mad."

Instead of being a question, it served as a statement. Normally, people would ask, but it was not necessary with Thelma and her psychic skill. It might be easy to joke about her mind-reading ability. It wasn't exactly that but more like simple impressions. More than once, Donna had met people who struck her the wrong way and tried to logically talk herself around it, only to find out later they *were* bad news. Obviously, her peevishness at being closed out of the case showed.

"I'm not upset about the glasses. I buy that stuff at the dollar store. It looks decent and doesn't hurt my bottom line. It only took me six weeks to figure out guests bust up stuff. I had to consider where to invest my money as far as furnishings."

"Okay." Thelma flashed an uncertain smile, gave Jasper a final belly rub, and then stood. "If not the glasses, then what?"

Should she say anything? Her husband preferred to keep things close to his chest. Even Donna wasn't a fan of airing family dirty laundry. It wasn't exactly dirty laundry—unfair laundry, maybe. Besides, Thelma either could guess it with her psychic skills or had overheard their discussion.

"Howard gets to go to work with Mark." She emphasized the next two words. "*In fact*, Legacy's finest is overjoyed to hear what pearls of wisdom will fall from his mouth."

Donna rested the broom against the wall but still had a grip on the now-empty dustpan. She slammed it against the counter.

"It makes you mad. I can understand that." Thelma nodded her head, put her fists on her narrow hips, and continued. "No one ever asks me for my help, and I practically solved the last murder."

"Ahem," Donna cleared her throat, crossed her arms, and gave her helper a pointed look.

"I'll admit you helped."

If stares could be measured in Fahrenheit, Donna's cool one dropped the room temp about ten degrees, triggering Thelma, who sputtered, "*You helped a lot.* If I hadn't come by and told you murder was in the air, you wouldn't have bothered to leap into action."

Whenever crime happened inside the limits of their sleepy burg, Donna's natural curiosity, paired with her crime-solving ability, resulted in her giving the officials in charge often unasked for assistance. Instead of pointing this out, she shifted to tool number three in her bag of tricks: changing the subject. "I guess I'm mad because sometimes I feel like I'm in a 1950s sitcom. The men go out and do the dirty work, catch the criminals and stuff, while the little women stay home and knit or something."

"Sometimes, Legacy does feel like it's caught in a time warp." Thelma relaxed her belligerent stance, carried the dishes to the dishwasher, and loaded them as she spoke. "I thought there were a couple of women in the police department."

Donna turned to address Thelma as she inserted the dishes with a great deal of clanking. Good thing she didn't spend good money on plates. "I think there's two, maybe three, but I never hear Mark talk about them. I'm not sure what they get to do. Who knows? They could be making coffee and answering the phone."

She held up one finger. "I know one thing for sure. The commissioner acts like he's physically unable to listen to a woman. When I open my mouth, I might as well be Charlie Brown's teacher. All he hears is unintelligible sounds."

"I know what you mean," Elizabeth said from her spot in the open doorway.

A surprised Donna spun around. "I didn't hear you come in."

"Not surprised," she grinned. "Your husband and my husband are off for the day, fighting crime. That leaves me with you. From what I heard it sounds like things are about the same as they are back home."

The comment ended with a heavy sigh. "I was hoping things would be different over here. Heard my guy say you help your husband with your cases. I've tried. Had good insights, too, but no one will listen to me as just a civilian."

Her gaze slipped downward along with her lips. Even though they'd just met, the woman pulled on Donna's heartstrings. Despite her inability to recognize a proper British breakfast when she saw one, she made Donna want to do something special to cheer the gal up.

"Hmmm," Donna murmured to herself as a plan formed in her brain.

"Listen up." She cleared her throat, trying to sound a bit more authoritative. "The secret to helping out on a case is not asking for permission." Her index finger wagged as she continued. "No reason to since we know the reception we'll get. Don't worry your pretty, little heads. Let the professionals handle it."

"Ain't that the truth," Thelma inserted with vigor. "No one listens to my vital information, with the exception of Donna."

Elizabeth pressed her hands together in front of her chest. "I think I'm going to like this."

"You will," Donna asserted with confidence. "We're going to solve the murder. Once we do, we can lord it over our husbands, but first, we have to clean the kitchen."

Chapter Nine

THE SCENT OF burnt toast lingered like an uninvited visitor, while the kitschy cat wall clock with its swinging tail and rolling eyes clicked to ten o'clock. Donna turned on the dishwasher with a weary sigh. She untied her apron and addressed Elizabeth. "It usually doesn't take me so long to get cleaned up."

"Yeah," Thelma agreed and added, "All the extra dishes are a result of special breakfasts for certain guests."

For an alleged psychic, Donna's assistant missed the obvious, such as Donna not wanting to bring up the British breakfast fumble. Aware her guest might feel a touch of chagrin, Donna decided to pretend it hadn't bothered her. "No big deal. These things happen."

Not willing to give it up, Thelma did a double take. "You acted plenty hot when I came into the kitchen."

Before anything else might be said, Donna coughed and then nudged Thelma. "I believe you have some rooms to freshen."

Her helper blinked as if she'd forgotten part of her job consisted of tidying the guest rooms as opposed to repeating every careless word she'd overheard. "Oh, right. I'll get right on it."

Not trusting Thelma to not continue her conversational vein, she turned to Elizabeth. "Better go grab your purse. We need to hit the road."

"That's aces," Elizabeth cooed. Her glance went to the dishwasher that churned away. "You really should do something about those

45

demanding folks who keep you busy with all sorts of extras requests. I could talk to them."

"Oh, no." Donna flushed when she realized she practically shouted the words. Thelma arched her eyebrows as she drifted out of the kitchen. "No worries. I prefer to handle my own issues."

"Quite smart of you to do so." Elizabeth shot her an approving nod. "I heard Americans are straight forward."

Donna smiled, wondering how her guest would take the southern tradition of not saying what you're thinking, but speaking in code. Still, it was a code the other women knew. *Bless his heart* said in several different situations could mean anything from sympathy to softening the blow before an insult. Often, certain words meant the exact opposite. A bald man might be nicknamed Curly, while a heavy male could be called Slim. Many southern women referred to their aging husbands as a stud more as a courtesy than a fact. Precious could denote something small, darling, or lacking. It depended on the context and the speaker.

"Ah, yes. Some are straight shooters. The sooner you grab your bag, the sooner we leave. Make sure to think of some American things you want to do."

As Elizabeth hustled to get her purse, Jasper chose that moment to give her a suspicious look. "Yes, *I* am leaving. No, you can't…"

She stopped before completing the sentence. Many more places were allowing dogs. If they stopped for a bite, they could eat outside. As Donna eyed her dog, another super sleuth idea occurred to her. Something the professionals would never consider. Old dogs like Jasper relaxed people into saying more than they might when they encountered dogless individuals.

By the time she'd retrieved the leash from the key rack, her aging puggle stood and quivered with glee. She bent to snap on the lead as footsteps clattered down the stairs.

A breathless Elizabeth entered the room. "I'm back."

"So, I see. We'll use the side entrance."

Jasper, knowing the routine, pranced ahead, leading the way with Elizabeth serving as the caboose.

"You're taking your dog?"

The fact that Jasper led the way with a leash trailing behind should be self-evident, but often people asked questions even when presented with the obvious. "It'll help us find the murderer."

"Oh," Elizabeth uttered in awe, pressing her hands together. "Is he going to sniff out a trail?"

"He might." Amused that her pooch might do anything work-related, she forgot to add on the *sniffing out* he'd do depended on which restaurant they chose for the day.

They weaved their way through the narrow hall and out to the stoop. As they walked down the stairs, the bright sun had Donna reaching for her sunglasses to shield her eyes.

"Did you bring any shades?"

"What?"

Donna turned to face her guest and pointed to her sunglasses.

"Oh yes! I bought them at the airport." She pulled out heart-shaped glasses with a light rose tint and popped them on her face, resulting in her looking a bit like a pre-teen or eccentric—more likely the latter.

"Those might not be dark enough, especially with the light reflecting off the sea. I thought we might go to the Croaking Frog restaurant that sits along the seashore."

"Super," Elizabeth said with a wide grin. "Is it open all night? I've heard about restaurants being open twenty-four hours a day."

"Not here, you didn't. At the most, some of the more expensive restaurants might stay open till ten, but by then, everyone, except the help, has headed home."

"Oh…" The word came out in a gust, dripping disappointment.

Peculiar. "Why does it matter so much to go to an all-night restaurant?"

"It was on a list of things uniquely American."

"Huh," served as Donna's reply. It made her wonder who came up with this so-called list.

Their steps had carried them to the sedan. Donna dropped the leash to dig through her purse for the keys. Once found, she unlocked the doors with her fob. Elizabeth swung open the passenger door, setting off Jasper, who wiggled underneath the car, only to pop up on the other side and leap into the seat.

"Jasper usually rides shotgun," Donna commented to explain the dog's sudden burst of energy.

Her spoiled canine usually stayed home when Mark drove, which meant Jasper had no expectation of sharing the front seat or moving to the back. Her pooch settled into the seat with a smug turn of his loose doggy lips.

"Shotgun?" Elizabeth's brow puckered and she glared at Jasper, who paid no attention.

"Front seat," Donna explained. It wouldn't be easy making Jasper give up his position, but luckily, she had a few tricks up her sleeve. "Okay, we need Jasper. I'll explain more as we go. I'm going to have to fool him, and you're going to have to be fast."

With the back driver's side door open, Donna climbed in and crinkled a cellophane wrapped object. "Yum, yum, I have a delicious treat."

Jasper slowly turned his head, curious, but not buying it. That's the problem with a smart pooch. Donna clawed at the cellophane, trying to open the breadstick she kept in her purse for incidents like this. For Pete's sake. How did they expect people to get to the breadstick? When she resorted to tearing the package with her teeth, Jasper wiggled between the two front seats into the back, obviously intrigued.

A solid thump demonstrated Elizabeth's quickness in taking over the seat.

"Good job."

Donna gave her dog the now opened breadstick and a pat before slipping out of the back. As she buckled herself in, she considered Elizabeth had potential as a sleuth companion, but the woman needed to know a few things.

"Before we talk to anyone, I need to remind you to say nothing about the murder. The secret to being a sleuth is to ask mundane questions, allowing the people to relax. That's where Jasper comes in. People forget their barriers around pets. They'll often tell animals things they wouldn't tell their hairdresser or priest. All we have to do is listen but pretend we're not."

"The killer would confess his crime to your dog?"

"Not exactly."

Donna started the car and listened to the engine catch before switching on the air conditioning. The beginnings of a tension headache throbbed behind her left eye, forcing her to squint as she reversed the car. Did Elizabeth think with the magic of Jasper, they'd track down the killer and get him to confess in sixty minutes or less like on the crime dramas?

"Even dumb ones tend not to blurt out their deed until they've quaffed a few brews, and we don't know who the killer is. We're going to gather some clues and then tie them together and see what we come up with."

"I'm ready." Elizabeth rubbed her hands together. "What's next?"

Normally, Donna would tap into her mother's gossip network. She still planned to do as much while showing her newest guests around town. "What else is on your list of totally American things?"

"Fried food."

"Mercy, you hit the mother lode here. We have fried chicken, chicken fried steak, fried pies, fried biscuits, fried pickles, fried catfish, fried green tomatoes, fried okra, fried beignets—"

Donna had several more things to add, but Elizabeth interrupted her.

"What's a beignet?"

The question surprised her so much Donna tapped the brakes, resulting in jerking forward. "A little bit of heaven. You poor dear, never knowing the eggy, sweet goodness of a beignet still warm, melting in an explosion of flavors inside your mouth. We must remedy that."

"Brilliant!"

It just happened that Margery's love of the airy pastry had been common knowledge. Who knows? Maybe they'd pick up a clue or two along with the beignets.

Donna felt compelled to explain more on the basic rules of sleuthing. "First rule of sleuthing is to tell no one you're sleuthing. The second rule is everything can be a clue." Since they were headed to The Croaking Frog, Donna added one more. "Never discount the value of gossip."

Chapter Ten

THE MATURE OAKS created a leafy arch over the street, shielding the walkers from the glare of the strengthening summer sun. It also created a restful atmosphere, especially since large trucks were prohibited from using this street. In an effort to show Legacy's best side, Donna chose the area of town that featured restored homes with manicured yards, which gave away to sidewalk cafes, smart boutiques, and coffee bars that charged as much for a cup that a pound of beans would cost.

Donna pressed the button, lowering the windows. "You can hear the sea from here."

Her guest cupped her ear as her brow furrowed and said, "You're right," with a touch of astonishment in her voice.

Of course she was right. Why would Donna even mention it if it wasn't so? It was best to change the subject. "How do you help your husband with his cases?"

A chortle greeted the pronouncement. "Any way I can. However, when I make the mistake of saying something around the other officers about a dodgy character, they act like I'm daft. When my husband says the same thing, it's brilliant."

"I hear that. Give me some examples."

It might even give Donna possibilities she hadn't considered. Anything that could give her an investigator edge and demonstrate to the commissioner a civilian could be a big help, she'd grab with both hands.

Elizabeth started. "Well, there was a lonely heart scam going on. Women were meeting some lothario online who would flatter them and then hit them up for money. He insisted he lived in France and needed money to visit. Despite being wealthy, all his money was currently tied up in investment, inheritance issues, or some other financial nattering meant to confuse the average person. He promised to not only pay the money back, but to double the amount spent."

"Ah, greed," Donna remarked.

Her passenger returned to her narrative. "Howard brought home copies of the letters the man wrote. The general consensus was nothing could be done if the letters originated from another country. I read the letters and told him he wasn't from France, and it wasn't a male."

"How did you know?" During the recitation, she'd heard nothing that would indicate otherwise.

"Oh, you know how it is. No one wants to think someone in their own town or country would be the guilty party. Foreign criminals make everyone happy."

"Same here, except foreign could mean the next state. Go on," Donna encouraged as she turned toward the shore road that would take them to the beach and The Croaking Frog restaurant.

"The writer bragged about his job as an international diamond cutter and how he traveled around the world with his little dog— often jetting off just to watch a football game, but always taking his beloved pet. I knew then not only was he *not* a Frenchman but probably someone who didn't travel at all."

"Most people lie on the dating apps, but what was the giveaway? How about not being a guy?"

"The dog for the first part."

"You think he didn't have one. I imagine people lie about that, too. I read once that women preferred photos of men with dogs as opposed to men with cats."

"It wasn't the dog, per se. Nonetheless, I suspected he didn't have one. He was clueless that you couldn't travel from one country to the other with your pet. After the mad cow scare, pets have to stay in quarantine for at least ten days. It's up to six months in the UK. Why would anyone put their pet through that? His throwaway remark about flying off to see a game with his pet didn't ring true. I suggested they look a little closer to home and check out any connections to the women he managed to fleece."

Who knew an animal had to stay in quarantine so long? Donna gave her guest points for being in the know. The traveling diamond cutter occupation sounded bogus to her. "How did they nab the lonely heart lothario, or should I say, *her*? You never explained how you knew it was a her."

"Imagine," Elizabeth said and then chuckled, "the type of letter you'd like to receive. Something romantic along the lines of it's as if our minds reached across the miles and brushed one another. In the brushing, we realize we'd not only spent other lifetimes together but, in those lifetimes, loved like none other. Even the sun watched us in its jealous sky."

Using her free hand, Donna wafted the air in front of her. "Whoa. Seriously? The last bit sounded a tad like a song."

"Maybe. It's not word for word, but something like that. A bloke would say something short and blunt like, 'how about a snog?'"

"What?" As soon as the query was out of her mouth, Donna wished it back. Did she want to know what a *snog* was? It sounded disgusting.

"Kissing." Elizabeth leaned across the console to nudge Donna. "Movie kissing is what I call it. All hands everywhere, as if a few extra limbs had been added for the scene."

"Got it. We just call that kissing. How did you track down the culprit?"

A snort came from the passenger side of the car. "If it had been a pound or two, or even twenty, people would shrug and say that's life. We're talking life savings, recent inheritances, and all that."

Donna clicked her tongue and shook her head. "Makes me thankful I'm married, although I like to think I wouldn't be foolish enough to be pulled into such a scheme."

"Me, too. When it came down to the footwork, the bobbies went with the tried and true, looking for things they all had in common: addresses, schools, jobs. All Scotland Yard found was the victims had never attended school with each other, they didn't live close to one another, nor were they employed at the same corporation. I suggested hobbies, nail techs, favorite shops, and hair salons. Eventually, they found the culprit was a shampoo girl with great listening skills. Women tend to tell the stylist all sorts of secrets. Not only did Ava know which woman was online looking but she also knew what type of man they were hoping to meet. By creating a man of their dreams, they came to her. She romanced them for a few weeks before asking for funds via an online app. She said the dumb cows deserved it."

"Clever of her, but in a dastardly way, taking advantage of women who believed in the fantasy of the perfect man."

The sound of the waves grew louder as Donna turned onto the seashore lane. Beach umbrellas added color to the sand. An occasional playful squeal indicated a shore visitor found out the ocean tended to be colder than expected, even in the summer.

"You should make time for the beach. You could take selfies for your friends back home."

"I'm rather chuffed about it, but first, we need to solve the murder. Then we can play in the surf and work on my American list." She leaned out the open car window and inhaled. "Ah, the seashore. It's so refreshing."

"It can be," Donna agreed while musing over how she seldom took advantage of living on the coast. Tourists comprised the majority of shellcombers on the beach, while locals with young children still made an effort to visit the ocean. Teens often enjoyed the waves, but sometime after college they all became too busy to saunter barefoot through the sand. "What else is on your list?"

"Graceland, Elvis's home."

"That's not very close. Unless you want to spend twelve hours driving and twelve hours back. It's so popular you have to buy tickets in advance to visit on your desired day."

Donna felt like a huge meanie when Elizabeth's posture drooped at the information. The United States stretched over hundreds of miles, but it wasn't unusual for international visitors to want to visit Disneyworld, the Statue of Liberty, and then head out to the Rockies, or even see the Hollywood sign in just a few days. There had to be something she could do for missing out on the opportunity to stand beside Elvis's pink Cadillac for a selfie. "Ah, we might be able to squeeze in a secret Southern Woman ritual."

"Oh?" Elizabeth's voice swung up as she wiggled in her seat to face Donna. "What is it?"

Donna drove into the gravel parking lot of The Croaking Frog. A pithy saying about weaving a tangled web via lying came to mind. Still, Southern women had all sorts of traditions. Some involved potato salad, others sweet tea, and still others, the salon, the gossip mill of any town. After putting the car into park, she made eye contact with her passenger and held a finger to her lips.

"It's a secret. I'll have to see if I can make it happen. Until then, tell no one. Even after, it might be best to say nothing because it's a sacred Southern Woman tradition. Some things we don't want our menfolk knowing."

"Ooh." Elizabeth pushed out the word through pursed lips. "I can do. What now?"

"I happen to know that my mother and her cronies come here for brunch. As soon as I introduce you, they'll invite us to join them and then we'll listen to the gossip swirl around us. We might pick up some useful tidbits."

"Just like on the detective show, Delaney Jones. She's always getting invited to sit down and talk."

Donna wondered if Delaney had a grandfather named Barnaby but decided not to ask. She shouldered her purse and clicked her tongue at Jasper. "Ready to go, big boy?"

In response, Jasper gave two sharp barks. He sounded ready to her.

"Let's go."

The sunlight reflected off the waves, adding to the day's brightness. Even with her sunglasses on, Donna had to shield her eyes with one flattened hand as she made her way to the trunk and retrieved an orange service vest for Jasper. When she caught Elizabeth staring at it, she explained with an apologetic smile. "It's a sleuthing tool. I need Jasper to get the results I want. Hopefully, they'll be sitting outside. It's not like I'm going to parade my dog through the kitchen, although he'd like that."

The problem with beachfront restaurants was finding a piece of property sturdy enough to be the base. A slab of cliff served that purpose for The Croaking Frog. It was high enough to keep the place from being swept away by the tides. The customers ended up climbing a winding wooden staircase to enjoy the daily special. Thankfully, mobility-challenged guests had a series of parking spaces at the top. Even though they all had wheelchair icons painted on the blacktop, Donna knew that her friend Janice, the owner of the restaurant, painted over one of the spaces and used it, declaring that ownership should come with some perks. Walkers could access it by a cliff path. Her mother usually parked at a nearby friend's house and walked over to avoid the climb.

Too bad Donna didn't have any friends living nearby, considering she'd have to lug her pup up two flights of stairs. Carrying her thirty-pound puggle invalidated his service vest, but only if he were a guide dog. He could easily be a medical alert pooch, which she would definitely need by the time they reached the top.

"You go ahead, Elizabeth. Jasper and I will follow."

Light taps sounded on the steps as Elizabeth ascended. Perhaps Jasper would scramble up the stairs on his own. Donna put her foot on a step and tugged. Normally, her dog used the two steps from the side door to the yard, but he seldom used the steps to the second and third floors. He must have decided a while back nothing of interest existed up on the other floors.

"Come on, Jasper. You can do it."

One paw went up on the step, then the other. Jasper's butt made contact with the ground, and he rested his head on the front paws on the steps. He yawned and closed his eyes. Mercy. While she knew sleeping happened to be his major talent, she never thought he'd go asleep mid-step.

No help for it, she'd have to carry him. She blew out a breath before reaching down and lifting him. Most folks might cradle their precious pooch like a baby, but they had lightweight dogs. She slung Jasper's front paws over her shoulders and wrapped her arms around his waist. "Of all the cotton-picking ideas…"

"Did you say something?" Elizabeth inquired in her accented voice.

"No. Keep going. I'll catch up." She pushed out the words, trying not to sound too breathless. "Wait for me at the top."

A woman in a large-brimmed hat drifted to the side of the balcony that surrounded the restaurant. "Donna, is that you?"

Ah good, her mother was here. "It's me."

"Thought so," Cecilia called back. "Is that my fur grandson?"

Since Donna married late, she never provided her mother with grandchildren. The result was she dubbed Jasper her fur grandson. Her former assistant, Tennyson, was referred to as her surrogate grandson. Since her mother spoiled Jasper outrageously, he adored her. Just hearing her voice sent him into a wiggly frenzy, forcing Donna to put him down or lose her own balance. As soon as she did, the puggle raced up the stairs, pushing past Elizabeth in the process.

Her mother stood at the landing all smiles but was joined by a redhead garbed in a cook's apron. She scowled down at them. "Who's responsible for this flea-bitten mutt?"

Chapter Eleven

THE ROAR OF the ocean served as white noise for the diners. The Croaking Frog restaurant perched on an overhanging cliff that allowed a breath-taking view of the calm ocean and beach visitors below. The opinionated owner stood at the head of the stairs with her fists on her hips, inquiring about Jasper's presence. The friendly pooch recognized Janice and gave her a hopeful glance with his tongue lolling out. Staying in role, Janice refused to pet the dog and glared in Donna's direction.

Not too surprisingly, her back foot hanging frozen in the air, Elizabeth stood posed on one step, shooting a nervous glance a half-dozen steps behind at Donna. Her friend, Janice, could be intimidating when she chose to be. Just ask her employees.

All conversation stopped and heads turned toward what they assumed would be an unfolding scene and a hot piece of gossip. Donna sneered in her friend's direction. "That's no way to talk about my medical alert dog. We'll stay on the balcony."

Janice brushed her hands together as if ridding them of something and snorted. "Make sure you do."

The assembled diners watched her amble back to her kitchen before transferring their attention to the newcomers. Cecilia knelt and patted Jasper, who greeted her with generous tongue swipes. "I miss my little darling." Still kneeling, she addressed Elizabeth. "Hello! I don't believe we've met."

Donna scampered up the stairs the best she could, worried somehow her mother might say something a bit personal. An online blog mentioned the Brits could be a stickler for personal boundaries. This not only included personal space but also not asking about personal matters such as what a person did for a living. The article went on to say that many English people had remained friends for years and had never known their friend's occupation. Initially, when Donna read the article, her mind jumped to the possibility of never knowing if your bestie worked as a con artist or hitwoman.

Her mother might choose the other option, which would be to enlighten Elizabeth on the town's various secrets. She might even mention an amusing anecdote from Donna's childhood, except only her mother would view the humiliating episode as funny. In situations such as this, her mother often went with the exploding egg incident, which cast shade on her cooking abilities. Another favorite happened to be the rum ball incident when a twelve-year-old Donna thought she could dance after consuming too many rum balls at a community event. The answer was she couldn't.

With a determined effort, she dashed up the last few steps as Elizabeth replied. "Oh, hello. I'm Elizabeth. My husband and I—"

Before she could elaborate, Cecilia straightened, clapped her hands together, and gushed, "You're English! How wonderful. Come sit at my table. I'd be in heaven just listening to you read the local newspaper aloud."

"Why would I do that?"

Donna reached the porch, and her mother pointed to her table, which included her recent husband Simon, the debonair charmer who had fallen for Cecilia decades before and finally won her heart. He saluted Donna with a coffee cup. Actually, dining with one's spouse did happen, but it put a crimp in the initial plan to harvest the gossip fields.

Her mother threw over her shoulder, "Come along, Donna. Don't loiter."

Jasper padded behind his grandmother, dragging his leash, and possibly raising a few suspicions among diners about what type of medical alert dog abandons his human. They knew plenty of local ladies carried their small, fluffy dogs into friends' homes, hair salons, and even stores, although the local pastors drew the line at church services. The ladies of Legacy loved their dogs.

They all settled into their chairs and an attentive server showed up with a menu. "Sweet tea and a bowl of water for my dog," Donna said without consulting the menu.

Her guest, on the other hand, not only read it but pulled out her camera and snapped a photo, too.

The server, sensing an opening said, "We have a refreshing mint tea, a hand-squeezed lemonade, and a Southern Lemonade."

Janice had mentioned the addition of the last one, which was more of a cocktail made with lemonade, vodka, bourbon, and limoncello liquor. So far, it had been extremely popular this season.

Elizabeth's expression brightened, and she announced, "I think I will go with the Southern Lemonade."

The server smiled and then left.

Simon raised his eyebrows briefly but said nothing. Typically, the man seldom got in a word edgewise when surrounded by the women in the family. Still, he managed to convey a great deal with facial expressions.

Donna explained the unasked question. "Elizabeth is on vacation with her husband."

"Oh." Simon nodded, stood, and offered his hand. "Remiss of me not to introduce myself. Simon Lightwater and my beautiful bride, Cecilia."

Her step-father possessed old-world charm that used to be a feature for foreign characters in black and white films. Unlike the characters, he wasn't acting.

Elizabeth took his hand and inclined her chin. "My pleasure."

"Mine, too." Simon released her hand and retook his seat.

Cecilia launched into a series of questions, inquiring about the royal family, the flight, and her impression of the US so far. Any detective bent on the third degree would have been humbled by the rapid-fire delivery.

Donna held her hand up. "Mother, please."

"Too much?"

"Absolutely"

Elizabeth chimed in, "I don't mind. I realize Americans are known for being brash and asking impertinent and unimportant questions. I'm okay with it."

The glass Cecilia almost had to her lips met the table with a thunk. Her mother probably thought of herself as a gracious southern belle as most southern women did. She even referred to herself as the *iron fist in the velvet glove*. Her guest peeled off the velvet, much to her mother's chagrin. Simon mimicked a yawn, allowing him to cover his face with his hand, hiding his amusement.

Donna laughed instead, earning a censorious stare from her mother. Perhaps not understanding the reactions, Elizabeth repeated her earlier sentence. "I'm okay with it. I'd love to answer your questions."

Her mother's brow smoothed, her momentary embarrassment forgotten. "Great. The Queen?"

"Always a hard one. I can't remember there not being a queen. She's like a distant relative you know of but do not know personally."

A perfect British answer. Her mother beamed, probably unaware that while Elizabeth had technically replied, she'd said nothing good or bad about the queen, using the relative simile. Ask any American about the President and most would give you an earful, letting you know exactly where they stood while knowing even less about the person, they were referring to than Elizabeth did the Queen.

Their waiter returned with their drinks, which allowed everyone some welcome refreshment. Jasper slopped his water over the side of the dish—never a neat drinker.

Elizabeth took a healthy swig of her drink. "Delightful."

Okay, maybe she did tipple in the daylight. Donna had been a faithful watcher of the television miniseries of trials and tribulations of an aristocratic British family, and the one thing she remembered, besides the numerous clothes changes for various events, were the grand meals that included several courses with various wines. It amazed her the women remained rail-thin, and everyone managed to stay upright. Perhaps this was Elizabeth's heritage. It would stand her in good stead if she were in a pub soliciting information.

Right then, she needed details on Margery. After a murder, neighbors milled about, saying how nice the recently deceased was or how the suspect did charity work in his free time. Ten minutes later, the dirt started coming out with the mention of threats, affairs, and shady business deals. Donna wanted to make sure she managed to eavesdrop on the scandal mongers. "So, Mother, I'm surprised to see you here without your posse."

Her mother's light laugh—like wind chimes floating on the sea breeze—sounded. "Posse! I love it. I thought I'd spend time with Simon. Besides, I'll see them later at the emergency Garden Club meeting, which we had to convene due…" Her mother glanced both ways, leaned forward, and whispered. "…due to the murder of

Margery."

Emergency meeting. She needed to be there. Stuff would go down. Rumors would be dug up, and pretty much every townsperson would be examined to see if they had reason to snuff out Margery. About ninety-five percent would be malicious gossip since almost everyone had an ax to grind. It would take someone who knew the citizens and their various grudges, which would be her mother, and an experienced ear to separate fact from hearsay. Donna could perform the last. Now, all she had to do was get invited to the meeting.

The slurping sound of a straw reaching the bottom of the glass drew her eyes to Elizabeth, who grinned. "I must have been thirsty."

An attentive server swooped in and replaced the empty glass with another drink. Janice prided herself on service, but most locals knew to stick a spoon in the glass to indicate no refill. Tourists who got charged for the extra drinks possibly left whiny reviews, but The Croaking Frog served as the only seashore restaurant for miles, which is what vacationers wanted.

Donna caught the eyes of the server and held up her hand. "Bill, please. We'll be leaving soon." Turning to her mother, she added, "I need to be in that meeting."

"What about me?" Elizabeth questioned.

"You're right." Donna cleared her throat. "I meant *we* need to get into that meeting."

"Not sure how." Cecilia shook her head slowly. "It's a closed meeting. No new members. We won't even be talking about gardening."

"I know," Donna said, wondering why her mother didn't see the obvious. A crime needed to be solved. Possible clues dangled within reach *if* she attended the meeting.

Simon arched a brow as she spoke and asked, "What if you brought refreshments? Don't you always have refreshments?"

"Normally, yes," Cecilia agreed. "No time to make anything. I guess we'll do without. Besides, with Margery dead and all, it should be more of a somber meeting." She sighed and gazed off to the sea.

It was an opening, and her stepfather just created one just large enough for Donna to cram her size nine shoe into. "Margery *loved* sweets."

Sure, it was a guess, but the deceased could be described as curvy so she might have liked the occasional cookie or teacake.

"She did," her mother admitted softly and then swung her attention to Donna. "Scones, crumpets, all the English tea things. Bring enough for twenty. Library. One o'clock. In the Gracious Ladies' meeting room."

Elizabeth, who had been watching the exchange with great intensity, asked, "What do I do?"

She'd have to do something to explain her attendance at the meeting. "Umm…" Donna stalled as she cast about for possibilities, but Simon stepped in once again.

"You can be her helper."

"Crikey" Elizabeth announced with a tad too much enthusiasm. "Finally, I have my first undercover assignment."

Chapter Twelve

Donna's plan to bring the dog to the restaurant to get Margery's friends to spill their guts failed horribly due to the friends not being there. Now she'd have to rush home and make all sorts of goodies. On the way to do so, she'd have to carry her heavy pup down the stairs.

A playful shriek coming from the beach meant at least one person was enjoying the day. Unfortunately, it wasn't her.

"Tick, tock," her mother said, pointing to her watch.

"I know." Her mother's reminder had Donna holding up her bill folder with her credit card sticking out to flag down the server. Normally, she wouldn't resort to such aggressive behavior. Wanting service immediately earned a censorious look in the South. Only Yankees rushed around demanding to be served, which didn't make any sense being on vacation and all.

"Sweetie," her mother started, "there's no reason to forget your manners entirely."

"Yes, there is. I have to haul Jasper down the stairs, drive home, whip up some amazing goodies, and then show up at the library in less than two hours." Even verbalizing the list tired her.

Simon lifted his index finger, trying to get into the conversation. "Why not stop off at the grocery and pick up some cookies?"

Both Cecilia and Donna turned shocked faces his way. Southern women judged each other on their baking ability. At least, those of a

66

certain generation did. In Donna's case, her delicious refreshments served as her calling card, helping people decide to book the inn for their function or a getaway weekend.

Unaware of his mistake, Simon blinked and asked, "Did I say something wrong?"

Both women remained silent, leaving only the sound of slurping as Elizabeth polished off her second Southern tea. She grinned at the three of them. "Think I have time for another?"

Without planning to, Simon, Cecilia, and Donna said, "No," almost in unison, causing her hopeful expression to slip a little.

"No reason to be cheeky about it."

"Sorry," Donna apologized and added, "We're on the clock and need to get back as soon as possible. It would help if my car was on this level instead of hiking down to the beach. Sure, would be nice if my car was on *this* level."

Surely Simon would take the hint and move her car for her. Instead of her stepfather, Elizabeth stood up, weaving slightly before steadying herself. "I can move it."

Not in a million years would Donna allow someone new to the area and used to driving on the left side of the road to take charge of her vehicle. A wrong turn could result in driving into the ocean. Before Donna could defer treading the dangerous balance between truth and not offending her guest, her mother intervened.

"Go on. We'll take Jasper home with us. It'll be good for our dog, Loralee, to socialize. After the meeting, we'll run him by."

"Sounds good," Donna acknowledged while handing off her bill folder to the server. Not wanting to hurt her guest's feelings, she nodded in her direction. "I appreciate your offer to drive, but not today. Maybe another day."

"I can't wait!" Elizabeth patted the table in her enthusiasm.

"That's another thing on my American list. I hope we have time to do everything, including the special secret Southern Woman mystery ritual." As soon as the words were out of her mouth, she gasped, her eyes darting in Simon's direction, covering her mouth with a hand.

Biscuits and gravy! The woman apparently didn't have a head for liquor like all those aristocrats on those fictionalized British dramas. Her mother's eyebrows arched, demonstrating she'd caught the reference and would ask later. Just as well. If someone could concoct a sacred Southern Lady ritual, it would be her. Simon's attention dropped to his phone where he probably checked on sports scores or tried to watch a golf tournament on the three by five-inch screen.

A FEW MINUTES later, Donna rushed to turn on the stove and pull out ingredients while her guest perched on a stool, watching. Most might have encouraged Elizabeth to participate, and Donna might have if she'd had a larger time window. She needed something noteworthy, and that took time.

The kitchen door swung open as Thelma backed in, struggling with a laundry basket piled high with sheets. When she turned and saw them, she stumbled but caught herself and said, "I sensed something had changed."

No reason to point out the noise from Donna banging around the kitchen had telegraphed her location. All the same, she explained. "I have to whip up some treats for the gardening group in less than two hours."

"That's a problem," Thelma agreed and then placed her basket on the island. "Why don't you use tonight's goodies for the reception?"

"Good idea." Donna had forgotten she'd made everything ahead to deal with her VIP guests. A hazelnut strawberry tart, garden tomato salad, melon skewers, cold jumbo shrimp, and a double batch of macadamia chocolate chip cookies waited in the sub-zero fridge. "I could whip up a gallon of sweet tea and another of lemonade. Add in some nuts and mints and I should be good."

Elizabeth, who maintained her seat on her stool, interjected, "Also, maybe some Southern lemonade?"

"Probably not," Donna said.

The possibility of tipsy ladies might result in rattling a few skeletons in a closet but not necessarily the ones she needed. Besides, her reputation as the owner of the B and B where guests checked in and a few never checked out needed no more embellishment. Her nose crinkled as she considered her mother's comment about Margery loving all things British. She exhaled audibly.

"Margery preferred all things British."

"Sharp gal," Elizabeth offered, swinging her feet back and forth, rather like a young child.

"Not really." Thelma disagreed. "She only started saying that after everyone began binge watching all the British shows."

Most of Thelma's predictions were vague, allowing plenty of room for interpretation in her favor, but this seemed oddly specific. "Did the spirits tell you this?"

"No, Margery did."

Was Thelma a medium, too? Donna counted out napkins stamped with the Painted Lady Inn name as she wondered how to ask without sounding like the disbeliever she was. "Ah, she came to you in a dream?"

"Oh, no. Margery told me herself when she was alive. I've had many jobs over the years, and one of those was being hired to spring clean her house." Her eyes rolled upward before she added, "It may have been last year. Anyhow, I'm shining her silver tea service, and she tells me she's tired of all the British teas she hosted and could live without eating another cucumber sandwich for the rest of her life."

"Don't care for cucumbers myself," Elizabeth offered. "Fortunately, there's usually something else to nosh on at tea."

Margery got her wish not to partake in another cucumber sandwich, Donna mused, while realizing she might have an informant in her own kitchen. Even though she'd already promised to deliver goodies to the library, her heart beat a little faster with the possibility of unearthing the needed clues within her own inn.

Trying not to show her excitement, Donna assumed her best poker face and asked, "Anything else interesting happen while you were there?"

"It's hard to remember. I've done so many jobs. As clients go, she was an easier one. Not a hoarder and not a yeller, either." She shrugged her shoulders. "Could have been worse."

That was no help at all. She expected something more like a cloud of doom hovered over the home or an uneasy spirit roamed the hall. Something along that line. Even though Donna never solicited opinions on disturbances in the atmosphere, she'd make an exception today. "You intuited nothing?"

Thelma's hand went to her throat as her eyes took on a thousand-year stare. "Oh, the best way I can sum it up is she cared about appearances, and everything wasn't as she portrayed it."

Mercy. That described practically everyone in town. Donna fought the impulse to roll her eyes but failed. "Anything else? I mean, that's not much to go on."

"Ah…" Thelma said. She held up her index finger and closed her eyes.

Elizabeth's perplexed gaze went from Thelma to Donna, wordlessly asking what was happening. A little embarrassed, Donna knew she'd have to say something. She cleared her throat and whispered, "I think she's connecting to the spiritual world."

"Really!" Her slumped posture straightened, and her eyes brightened. "Brilliant! It's like I'm on that medium television show."

Not quite. On the show they had a clue what they were doing and managed to accomplish it in less than an hour. Thelma, instead, swayed a little, forcing Donna to step closer to be prepared to catch her if need be. Good help was hard to find, especially for the modest benefits she offered. An eerie, somewhat ghostly moan escaped Thelma's lips before she said, "Rival."

"What?" Did she say something about rye?

Thelma's eyelids popped open, and she enunciated very clearly. "Rival. I said rival."

"Does that mean she was killed by a rival?" Elizabeth asked. She leaned forward on the island, grinning triumphantly as if she'd personally wrapped up Margery's murder on her own.

It would be wonderful if that were the case, but most of Thelma's clues from the other side tended to be a bit like a conversation heard from a distance with nothing being too clear. Rather than disappoint either woman, Donna decided to go with it. "We'll have to figure out who Margery's rivals are."

Chapter Thirteen

A CART WOULD have been useful for getting the food from the inn's van up to the meeting room on the second floor of the library. Winded by the third trip, Donna made sure to exhale hard when she passed the reference librarian. The very same woman refused to allow them to use the elevator, insisting they looked healthy enough to handle the stairs. She even had the nerve to say the exercise would benefit them.

As far as healthy, it might be debatable. No wonder she never offered to cater events outside the inn. Some part of her must have known it would be something like this. Normally, she offered samples of her goodies to all she met, but Miss You Need the Stairs might miss out.

Donna entered the long, narrow room made so by a partition that could be added or removed to make the meeting room larger or smaller as needed. Laughter and soft conversation could be heard from the other side of the temporary wall.

Thelma and Elizabeth stopped in the anteroom and arranged the food. The spiked lemonade had melted any British reserve that Elizabeth might possess. After she had bragged about being the undercover assistant, Thelma shot Donna hurtful glances similar to Jasper when told he wasn't coming. In the end, she'd invited Thelma to assist.

Even though she hadn't initially planned on taking Thelma, it worked. Her assistant knew how Donna liked things laid out, which is more than she could say for her undercover helper. Elizabeth did very little work but had insisted on a disguise. Fortunately, Donna had found a left-over box of shirts Maria had made with an image of the inn. Above the inn was *Visit The Painted Lady Inn*. Underneath, it read, *We're Glad We Did*. Often, people wanted gifts from their stay but obviously, not those shirts.

Elizabeth donned her shirt with more enthusiasm than Donna expected. It could serve as a souvenir of her visit to Legacy, too. Right now, her British visitor made a fan of the napkins and laid a single fork on each napkin by grabbing the tines on each utensil. As a former nurse, Donna cringed.

"Wait!" she called, putting down her heavy box. She went over to help Elizabeth. "Here in the South, we put the forks tine side down, into a cup."

"Oh." Elizabeth picked up the forks again, handling them by the business end before inserting them into a cup.

Donna inhaled deeply, hoping that, like farmers, gardeners had great immune systems. After all, tons of articles espoused how people on farms were healthier than most due to their childhood exposure to livestock. Donna tried to reassure herself, not knowing what else to do about the much-handled forks. Running off with them to the restroom might cause some comment. By the time she could extract her antibacterial wipes from her purse, the ladies would be meandering into the room and spot her. Not exactly the reputation she wanted for the inn.

Lace tablecloths draped over floral tablecloths struck the right mood for her lady gardeners. Thelma had set out the food in the order it would have normally been served. The napkins and utensils rested next to the china plates. No one of quality would resort to paper plates unless for a barbeque, an unwritten rule among ladies of a certain age. After lugging the plates up the stairs, Donna felt paper plates would serve perfectly well—especially those fancy ones.

The door set in the partition wall creaked open. Cecilia slipped through it and closed it. "Wow! It all looks great."

"Thanks, Mom."

Donna smiled and rested her hands on her aching lower back. All mothers and daughters wrestled to some extent with their relationships. Theirs was better than most, but her mother often couldn't resist tweaking whatever her daughter did. Knowing this, she watched her mother close one eye and hold out her thumb in front of her as if surveying the scene.

"It's missing something," Cecilia said with certainty and an affirmative nod as if agreeing with her observation.

Naturally, her mother always *found* something. Trying not to show her frustration, Donna asked, in what she assumed wasn't a terse tone. "What?"

Cecilia wagged a finger in her direction. "Temper, temper," her mother teased. Her gaze returned back to the table, and she moved her outstretched hands, making a square. "It needs flowers. After all, it *is* a gardening group."

"I'm a caterer, not a florist."

Elizabeth abandoned her holding up the wall position and left the room. Part of Donna wondered about her exit but assumed she went in search of the facilities. How much trouble could a person get into in a library?

Her mother grimaced. "I know that. A big, framed photo of Margery would work, too. Something like 11x18, double matted, ornate frame."

"Seriously?" Her hands found purchase on her hips. Did her

mother even listen to herself? She doubted even Margery had such a photo in her own home.

Her mother grinned. "I guess you didn't happen to bring one with you." Her attention shifted to behind Donna as she announced, "Perfect!"

Curious to see what caused such an announcement, Donna turned to see Elizabeth enter, cradling a floral arrangement that looked slightly familiar. Her mother hurried forward, directing Elizabeth to the space that needed something. A white card popped against the glossy green leaves. Donna reached for it, wondering if it would detail the actual recipient.

The card read *Condolences on the death of Beau.* Good heavens! Someone else had died in Legacy, too. Before she could put the card back, the ladies entered, chatting. Donna slipped the card into her pocket and took her place by the very heavy thermoses of lemonade and sweet tea.

When serving at events such as weddings, showers, or even her own Friday reception, Donna soon discovered she was the help. At first, this distinction annoyed her, but she soon realized people talked freely in front of her, treating her as if she were deaf, except when they needed a refill on their drink.

Sweet tea sloshed over her hand as she passed out beverages. Chatter about the food washed over her. Normally, Donna enjoyed folks oohing and ahhing over her creations, but not today. Where was the gossip?

Due to her research, she recognized one of Margery's neighbors. Linda, a middle-aged woman, carried a few extra pounds padding out her waistline. With ash-blonde hair to hide the onset of the gray, a description of her could pertain to half the women there. Some-how, the neighbor featured in the discovery of the body, which made her a person of interest. However, Mark hadn't interviewed her personally, which meant the interest was minimal at best. Not too many murderers stuck around to find their own victims.

As the woman moved closer, she carried on a conversation with Cecilia. Knowing where Donna's interest lay, her mother prompted in a sotto whisper, "I heard Margery's husband was involved in an affair."

The neighbor snorted as she added cookies to her plate. "An affair? That would imply *one* female. I have it on good authority he had three women on the line."

Three women! Donna schooled her face so as not to reflect her surprise or even that she was eavesdropping. She moved her head the slightest bit, encouraging her mother to continue. Most people wouldn't clam up when given such a juicy morsel. In that regard, her mother persevered, "Any local girls?"

"Good Heavens, no. Any Legacy women would know he was married."

Donna mentally added, they'd also know his philandering ways. Three women complicated things. When the police investigated the spouse for the death of a wife, a girlfriend on the side usually existed. Often, the spouse committed the murder, while other times, it was the girlfriend, who wearied of waiting for the promised divorce. Sometimes they did it together.

Three women changed that dynamic. It could be that he had one solid mistress and the others were also-rans. On the other hand, gossip could just be gossip, too.

Chapter Fourteen

THE EMERGENCY GARDEN Club meeting ended with a vote on gardenias for the funeral and a small scholarship in Margery's name. Due to her mother leaving the door open, when they returned to the meeting after gathering their goodies, Donna could overhear almost everything.

What she couldn't do was move or make any type of noise that would alert them to the open-door situation. She held a finger to her lips, making sure both Thelma and Elizabeth witnessed her gesture. Did they use the same gesture in the UK? Maybe so, since neither helper spoke, but instead, wordlessly took a seat and retrieved their mobiles from their pockets.

Sleuths had no downtime to play games on their phones or shop. Instead, they listened and they watched. Unfortunately, Donna couldn't point this out since it would involve talking. She listened, slightly reassured her mother was doing likewise inside. Voices carried through the door.

"We should start a food train."

Several voices replied at once creating a conversational chaos for an eavesdropper. A few of the voices carried a low dissatisfied tone, more like the reaction when you're served fish at a wedding reception when you ordered steak. The rumble quietened, allowing one lone voice to ring out.

"Not sure why we'd do that. It's not like the *grieving* spouse will be at home."

Even though Donna couldn't see the speaker, it sure sounded like she had put air quotes around the grieving part. Jeff's wandering ways weren't a secret to most folks in town. Certainly, Margery had known. People married for different reasons, and their motives for staying together varied, too. Older couples often stayed together for companionship as opposed to love. Donna didn't really see companionship being a thing since Jeff happened to be gone more than he was home. Like most of the ladies of a certain age, Margery enjoyed her clubs, lunching with friends, weekly gossip at the salon while getting her hair done, and church on Sunday. It made Donna wonder what purpose a husband served in her life.

The ladies lobbed the idea of a food train back and forth for several minutes while Donna speculated on who was Margery's closest friend. Voices became heated again since bringing food to the family of the deceased was a time-honored tradition. It didn't matter if the spouse imagined himself the reincarnation of Don Juan. Tradition mattered. After a spirited discussion, they agreed to bring dishes to the funeral parlor's dining room where guests and family would enjoy a respite from the viewing room. It also served as a place where people renewed acquaintances long dormant and even laughed over memories.

The parlor kitchen provided an opportunity to nail down who was Margery's BFF. Donna pursed her lips, knowing her chances were about fifty-fifty. Strangely, once a person died, especially in a spectacular manner, folks claimed relationships that didn't exist and became the focus of attention while spinning tales about how close they were.

Donna would pay good money if just once, the deceased sat up and declared, "I have no clue who this person is. Stop acting like you know me!" Of course, if the deceased could do that, there would be no point to being in a casket unless it was a fake funeral. A few people faked their death to get out of a suffocating relationship, to escape financial obligations, or even to garner insurance money. The bullet to the head automatically eliminated Margery from such shenanigans.

Still, the funeral might provide an opportunity to identify friends. While most would admit to indulging in a little gossip, being nosy crossed a line. This meant a delicate inquiry would be needed. No help for it, she'd have to attend the funeral. Mark would have the details.

Someone mentioned they'd need to call the florist immediately because the funeral would be the next day. Donna blinked. *The next day.* Mercy! The man couldn't put her in the ground fast enough. It didn't make the husband sound especially heartbroken.

Donna blew out a breath through pursed lips, realizing while the hurry-up funeral might look bad, there might be some religious requirements that the deceased had to be interred in under forty-eight hours. It could be the result of attending that new church on the edge of town. A few town gossips even hinted that the deceased had to be buried standing up. That part, Donna doubted. Besides, Margery didn't have children who'd be coming in for the funeral, which meant no reason to delay the interment. All she had was a Maltese called June Bug that managed to get into more places than Jasper did.

There was so much to do, including cleaning up, fixing food to replace what they'd used, doing something American for Elizabeth, and making a dish to carry to the funeral. Her four-cheese macaroni screamed comfort food. No one wanted gourmet delicacies at a funeral. Ordinary, filling, tasty food would do the trick, and lots of it.

The counter would be crowded with sugar cream pies, fried okra, fried chicken, green bean casseroles, biscuits, hush puppies, fried green tomatoes, and sweet potato casseroles encrusted with pecans, brown sugar, butter, and spices. Yep, her macaroni and cheese would offer some balance.

A gavel thudded, signaling the end of the meeting. The ladies came streaming out, casting hopeful glances in Donna's direction. A plate of cookies sat uncovered, and Donna knew the drill. She gestured to them. "Sure, wish y'all would take some cookies home to your husbands."

No Southern lady would admit to grabbing extra cookies for themselves and then gobbling them down in the car. Several gathered around the platter like ants at a picnic. Donna couldn't help noticing one of the members must have a half-dozen husbands who merited cookies. The women waved, a few acknowledged Donna by name, and a couple of women even thanked her.

The stragglers missed out on the cookies but were in a deep discussion about what they would bring to the funeral dinner. Usually, churches handled the details of such an event, but Jeff hadn't darkened the doorway of a church in decades. The two women drifted past Donna, not even glancing her way, when one said, "I'm going to bring the four-cheese macaroni. It's amazing. I got the recipe from the Painted Lady Inn."

The other woman said, "Can't wait to taste it. Better make two pans."

Someone was stealing Donna's recipes or possibly passing off inferior recipes as if they came from The Painted Lady Inn? She wasn't sure which one was worse. For a moment, her mission to unmask Margery's killer was forgotten when faced with her more personal mystery.

The clatter of silverware and dishes signaled that Thelma was loading up everything. It sure would be nice to be able to use the elevator. First things first, she turned to Elizabeth. "Where did the plant come from?"

"Out there." Her guest extended her hand in the general direction of the library.

Well, that could be anywhere since there were two floors of various rooms. Donna forced a smile. "Could you be a little more specific?" She pulled the card out of her pocket. "It's probably someone sad since they lost someone recently."

"Oh." Elizabeth dug her toe into the faded floral carpet and moaned. "Sorry, my fault. I just wanted to help. There's a counter outside with a desk behind it. The flowers were just sitting there." Her shoulders went up in a shrug. "No one was around. Besides, we're going to put it back."

Donna's mouth gaped as she realized she'd somehow just been clumped into misappropriating the floral arrangement. Nope, not happening. A couple of sliding steps put her closer to the petals procurer and would make her query less likely to carry. "That desk?"

She pointed through the open door where the reference desk resided along with absolutely no hope of securing the use of the elevator.

Elizabeth clenched her hands and nodded.

"Ahh…" Donna hissed the word while squeezing her eyes shut. No wonder the reference librarian wasn't in the best mood. Add in the fact that Elizabeth stole her condolence bouquet. Worse things happened to folks than their flowers doing a walkabout, but Donna made a point of not being part of those things. Good manners dictated she should do something to smooth over the social gaffe. She held up her hand. "Do we have a clean plate?"

Thelma handed her one. Having a busy sleuthing schedule that left no time for a leisurely lunch, Donna had squirreled away some yummies for the three of them. She put together a decent peace offering from the leftovers. They would have to be offered up to the reference librarian since decency demanded it.

Plate prepared, Donna motioned to Elizabeth to bring the plant, and the two of them approached the reference desk where the librarian sat and regarded them with the same pinched expression one might assume when spotting a palmetto bug inside the bathtub.

"Hi!" Donna offered with forced joviality.

"Hush," the woman offered and somehow managed a more disgruntled mien. "It's a library."

Rather than explain she knew, Donna offered the plate loaded with a generous helping of reception goodies. The mini lemon meringue pie glistened under the lights. "I thought you might care for some refreshments."

"Oh, I couldn't." She dropped her eyes to the plate. "I only eat a strict diet of 1000 calories or less per day."

That explained her attitude. "All right," Donna commented as she reached for the plate. "I'm sure I can find someone who might like them."

While she spoke, Elizabeth slid the plant back up on the counter as inconspicuously as possible. A metallic clunk and a shower of scrap paper left on the counter alerted Miss One Thousand. She calmly noted, "Oh, that's where it went. Glad Pamela stayed home today to grieve the death of her beloved parakeet, Beau. She wouldn't take kindly to her arrangement growing legs and walking away."

Beau was a parakeet, and not even her bird, which explained the lack of accusations. Donna felt she needed to explain. "She's from

Britain."

"Oh." The librarian's eyebrows arched up, and her lips tipped up into a smile. "I love all things English."

While Elizabeth and the librarian chattered on about Britain, Donna had to tote everything back downstairs. After relocating the plant, Donna didn't dare mention the elevator. Instead, she and Thelma fetched and carried, happy the boxes contained less this time around.

Thelma, when she wasn't in the grip of a psychic prediction, could sum things up in a no-nonsense matter. As they slid the last box into the vehicle, Thelma straightened and asked, "Where's your little helper?"

Good question. A better one might be how much damage control would be involved.

Chapter Fifteen

B ACK AT THE inn, Donna hustled around the kitchen, recreating the goodies for tonight's reception that she'd just served to the Garden Club members. The fridge closed under Thelma's hand, triggering Jasper to glance up hopefully but receiving nothing for his soulful expression. Even though a few hours existed before the reception, it still remained a time crunch, especially since she had no clue what could happen next.

Elizabeth perched on a stool, watching her host and her assistant buzz around the kitchen like wind-up figurines.

Donna hefted a melon, two cantaloupes, a couple of cartons of strawberries, and grapes onto the stainless-steel island. "I'll need two dozen fruit skewers. Everybody loves them, even the vegans."

Thelma groaned. "Couldn't we have picked up those at Happy Pig Grocery?"

"They wouldn't be fresh. The melon would already be on the squishy side. Besides, we have a local couple staying for their anniversary."

"Understood," Thelma acknowledged. She picked up a chef's knife and stabbed the watermelon, possibly expressing her frustration at having to make the time-consuming fruit skewer.

Elizabeth focused intently on the melon rind attack until it became obvious nothing more serious than melon balls would result. She glanced up and inquired with a furrowed brow, "What does a local couple have to do with anything?"

The answer was part of the intricacies of running a bed and breakfast she tried not to share with anyone outside the family. No reason to admit that locals would be quick to mention any subpar food. Even though most of her overnight customers weren't local, she did snag an occasional shower, ladies' tea, or wedding reception. She'd best change the subject. "What's your opinion of the husband being good for the deed?"

"Well," she hesitated and looked off in the distance. "Television would have us believe people are killed by random strangers, such as robbers, junkies, or some daft guy you cut off in traffic and followed you home. It might even be someone who held a grudge against you for decades, if you believe the telly."

The slight aroma of almost burning crust sent Donna sprinting to the oven. She pulled out the cookie sheet crowded with lemon tarts minus their meringue. As she relocated the tarts to the counter, Elizabeth recited practically every crime drama Donna had ever watched.

She decided to cut the conversation short. "What do *you* think?"

Elizabeth inhaled deeply and then asked, "Did I hear right that he had three lasses on the line?"

"Rumor has it," Donna concluded as she strained the egg whites for the meringue. With the crust a little more done than she liked, foil might be added for toasting the meringue. The egg whites slid into a commercial sized mixer bowl. Donna then added sugar and cream of tartar. Once she turned on the mixer, she stepped closer to hear Elizabeth say,

"Typical American..."

A derisive snort sounded. Thelma stopped melon balling and gaped open-mouthed.

Well aware of some of the crazy things foreigners believed about Americans, Donna arched her brows. "Nope. Might be a typical *fantasy* but not a reality. I find it hard to believe that about Jeff." She clucked to herself. "Some women can do some fool crazy things. Maybe there are three misguided souls out there."

"We need to talk to those three," Elizabeth offered with certainty and a definite head bob. "After we do so, we'll have a better feel if the man is guilty. Does anyone know where he is? Did he flee the country?"

"No," Donna answered, feeling a measure of pride in that she had inside information. She stepped back to scrape the bowl. "Such behavior would put the cuffs on him for sure. According to his secretary, he was in another state at a dental conference. He's home now, planning his wife's funeral."

The information caused Elizabeth to sit up a little straighter. "We'll need to drop by and see him."

Did she seriously think they could knock on Jeff's door and pepper him with questions about his late wife and his probable part in her murder? "You manage to do that in London?"

The possibility made Elizabeth laugh. "Of course not. I don't know the victims." Her eyes took on a shine as she placed both elbows on the island and leaned forward. "Surely there's something you can do. Tell him you want to know her favorite flowers. Maybe you want photos of her to put up at the funeral home or something. Maybe you want to make one of those videos that show up at weddings and funerals."

Good gravy! The Brit had come up with a decent plan before she did. The woman's sleuthing skills had just risen in Donna's estimation. "I'm not that good a friend of Margery's."

"Was he that good a husband?" Elizabeth queried with a knowing smile.

She had a point. "They had separate lives, not the usual type of marriage with the two engaging in shared activities. What are you getting at?"

Elizabeth straightened on her stool and pressed her hands together with a huge smile. "He wouldn't know who her friends were."

"It's possible." Plans took shape as she put a dollop of meringue on each tartlet. Maybe if she lowered the temp her crust wouldn't burn. If need be, she could use a torch to finish it off. "We can't trot over there without something to bring. Thank goodness I have a praline cheesecake in the freezer. There isn't anyone who would turn that down."

Sure, she had made the cake for Mark since it was his most favorite thing in the world. When he especially got down, cheesecake helped. Since he didn't know the cake existed, he couldn't miss it. With any luck, Jeff wouldn't be lactose intolerant. Even if he was, good manners dictated he'd accept the gift.

The problem with saying you are going to do something was you had to actually do it. "We should just ask for photos, then take them to the funeral home. A video is beyond my technical skill and sounds like work."

What she didn't add was she'd not like hearing others bash her feeble efforts, and they would. Donna couldn't take the blame or the credit for photos others took. "Sounds great, but first, we need to get the reception food done."

"Um…" Thelma cleared her throat and stopped creating melon balls. "Who will serve at the reception if you're out sleuthing?"

"I'm sure my mother will help."

Thelma muttered something about being even bossier than Donna.

Most people didn't recognize that trait about Cecilia. She epitomized Southern womanhood, oozing sweetness and platitudes while directing people to do what she needed to be done in a soft, genteel manner. Most gladly did it, unaware they'd been manipulated. The charm gene must have missed Donna. Fortunately, her razor-sharp intellect made up for her limited charisma. Sometimes, it took a little more to win over folks.

"Thelma, I realize you've gone beyond your usual duties. I'm appreciative." Even though she knew she'd regret it, she said, "What can I do to make it up to you?"

Maybe she'd ask for money, a special dish made for her, or an extra day off. Thelma blurted out, "Séance. I want to hold a séance in the front parlor."

Elizabeth echoed the word with bright eyes and a rapturous expression. "Séance! This trip keeps getting better and better. I imagined it would be a huge bore. A friend helped me make a list of American things to do so it wouldn't be a waste. Luckily, we have a murder to investigate."

Bore stuck out in glowing neon letters in Donna's mind. Instead of being excited about visiting the charming town of Legacy, Elizabeth thought it would be dull. The few upward steps Elizabeth had made in her esteem vanished. All the same, she promised Mark she'd keep Elizabeth entertained. Then, there was the possibility the two of them could solve the murder before the men.

"I'm glad we were able to provide a murder for your entertainment."

"You Yanks! Such jokers."

Thelma's head shot up, hoping to see Donna's reaction to the unwitting insult. Since this wasn't the first time, Donna didn't flinch. Instead, she smiled in Elizabeth's direction.

"If we want to get to the house before Jeff leaves for the funeral home, we'll need some help."

Her gaze drifted to the large sink piled with pans. Understanding the hint, Elizabeth slipped off the stool and headed for the sink.

Thelma gave her a questioning glance, possibly wondering why Donna didn't mention the dishwasher.

Chapter Sixteen

THE FRONT DOOR of the inn creaked open, piquing Donna's curiosity. A familiar British male voice made her forget about the trials of living close to a beach as Howard questioned Mark while the two entered the foyer. "You're certain the husband isn't guilty?"

Donna pushed the door open a little wider since the answer mattered. There was no reason to waste a good cheesecake if Mark knew the murderer.

"I didn't say that," Mark asserted and gave a low chuckle. "We have eyewitnesses that put Jeff Baumgarten and his pretty little assistant at the dental conference. He even presented at one point. Besides, his assistant would serve as his alibi, I bet."

Howard's eyes rolled upward as he stroked his chin. "He couldn't duck out of a meeting and drive home, kill the wife, and then return back to the conference?"

He must think the convention was the next town over. Always tactful, Mark cleared his throat. "I looked into it. It's a good eleven hours or more driving time. That's on a perfect day with no road construction, no wrecks, and pretty much no traffic."

"Airplane?" Howard asked the same question Donna would have.

"At least five hours because every flight goes through Atlanta. They say even after you die you have to go through Atlanta to reach heaven. There are no direct flights. With the increased security at airports, Baumgarten couldn't slip by. We'd have him on camera, and he has to present a legitimate ID to get through the security process."

"Private plane."

Another good question. She had to give it to Howard. Maybe the man did know his stuff.

"Checked. We don't have a close private airport. Jeff doesn't own an airplane or have a pilot's license."

It sounded as if Jeff firmed up his alibi. Most people, if asked, wouldn't have a great alibi. They might have returned home after work, ate dinner alone, watched television, and retired. At best, they could mention the show they watched. This used to be a way to check alibis, but with the ability to binge shows or re-watch old favorites, it no longer worked. Those who needed alibis made sure to be seen at events, held onto receipts to prove shopping locations, commented on social media, or called others to prove where they were. It wouldn't be too hard for a killer to call home before a crime to establish his alibi. Bold ones even attended a child's ballgame or school play after murdering a spouse.

Could Jeff be one of the bold ones? Donna must have spoken out loud because both men turned in her direction. Mark smiled, stepped closer, and pulled the door wider to dust a kiss on her cheek. He noticed the shoulder bag on her shoulder. "Hello, sweetheart. You headed out?"

"Just for a bit. I have some food to drop off for a funeral. Mom is coming by to start the reception if I'm not back in time."

"All right, then," Mark said, his shaggy brows pulling together a bit. "I'm sure you'll be back soon."

The hall bathroom door swung open, and Elizabeth exited in a cloud of perfume and gave her hair a final pat. "I'm ready."

"You're taking Elizabeth along?" Mark cocked his head and gave his wife a penetrating gaze, which Donna turned slightly to avoid and laughed.

"Of course! I want to expose her to American traditions. We'll be back soon." She gestured to Elizabeth, who waved at her husband before following Donna into the kitchen. The cheesecake sat on the island bundled up in a white cake box with a white ribbon.

As her hand reached for it, she heard Mark say, "Something's up, and I think your wife might be involved."

"That wouldn't surprise me. She tends to stick her nose where it doesn't belong."

Elizabeth stiffened beside her, but Donna gave her a nudge and held her finger to her lips. The two continued to move to the outer door where they were greeted by sea-tinged air as they exited.

THE GREEK REVIVAL home could have served as a stand-in for Tara in the *Gone with the Wind* movie, only the Baumgarten residence was better landscaped, not too surprisingly. The home had been in the family for three generations, which allowed the majestic oaks to grow to their full glory.

"Oh my!" Elizabeth exclaimed, peering out the car window. "This is just like some of the noble houses in England you can tour."

"I doubt it's *that* nice. Most of the houses in this neighborhood are on the garden tour. Once a year, if you buy a ticket, you can tour the extensive gardens that are heavily guarded by the owners and gardeners. I remember one harpy standing at the edge of her lilies, glaring at everyone. The owners possibly believed one of the great unwashed might step off the path, pick a flower, or snap a photo to recreate an especially cute flower bed or fountain."

"Surely they wouldn't mind a photo?"

"Depends. If it's to show off the garden to folks who could never have such a nice place, then that's acceptable. The real problem is other contestants stealing design ideas, which could be the reason they're taking photos. Often, relatives or spouses would be sent to do the photographing since they'd be less suspicious."

Donna's eyes rolled up as she visited her memory filing cabinet. "Oh, wait. They moved the date of the tour so that doesn't happen anymore. Once, two gardens had the same weeping angel statue, right by where Fluffy had been laid to rest. After that, the dates for the tour were pushed forward to prevent such a thing from happening,"

An unladylike snort erupted from Elizabeth. "Bloody daft if you ask me. Couldn't it be a coincidence?"

Here she thought the British took gardening very seriously. Most of the BBC's mysteries showed the women of a certain age bird watching, gardening, or running a tidy little tea shop. "No coincidences when it comes to garden competition." Donna rested her right hand on her chest. "I like to dig in the dirt, plant a few bulbs, and see what happens. Even so, I'm not ruthless enough to be part of the Garden Club. Not having tubs of money is an issue, too."

"Those women in the library acted like genteel matrons, ready to lend a hand if needed."

"Ha! In this case, you can't judge a book by its cover. As an out-of-towner, they'd be nice to you. You're not a threat. Neither am I, for that matter, but they would act much differently if they thought you were a rival. Stuff has happened in the past, including someone releasing dozens of snails into a prize-winning garden. I wouldn't be surprised if several of the members didn't take part in that chicanery."

"Whoo! Didn't Thelma mention a rival?"

Donna exhaled audibly, aware somehow that Elizabeth had gotten the jump on her. Then again, Elizabeth took Thelma's predictions seriously. Initially, Donna considered any *rival* to be of the romantic sort, but what if a gardening rival had done the deed? Oddly, it made more sense. After all, if a romantic rival was an issue, why had nothing happened until now?

"She did." Donna maneuvered the car around the circle drive and parked by the stone steps leading up to the front veranda. "We might want to ask for photos of Margery and friends to see if we can pick out potential rivals."

"Brilliant," Elizabeth acknowledged as she opened the car door, not waiting for Donna.

Their ability to get inside the house was slim to none, which would veer to the none if Elizabeth got to the door first. Even Jeff would know no Brits resided in Legacy. She wrenched open the back door, grabbed the cake, and then dashed to the stairs, trying not to jostle the box.

"Wait up!"

Elizabeth stopped on the steps and shot her an annoyed glance. In a few lunging steps, Donna drew even with her visitor and gasped, "I need to do the talking. I'm sure Jeff would recognize me. If not, I'll mention Mark. Everyone knows him. Sometimes, people tend to trust me more when they know I'm married to the town's premier detective or don't suspect me of doing anything peculiar."

"Lucky you."

She cleared her throat when the front door swung open. A tall man with shaggy dark hair tinged with silver and a softening jawline that gave testament to former handsomeness appeared. As Donna approached the door, the man blinked his red-rimmed eyes.

Curious. The normally dapper Jeff gave the appearance of grief. He must be the best actor ever. Truly, he had missed his calling.

"Hello, Jeff," she called out in a moderate soft voice. "So sorry for your loss."

"Thank you."

He rubbed his eyes and blinked again. "Should I be expecting you?"

Was he tired, grieving, drunk, or possibly all three? In any case, it was an opportunity. "Oh, we brought you a homemade praline cheesecake. You can freeze it if you have too much food." She offered the box, which he took. Afraid he might slam the door on them, Donna followed him into the house. "We came for the pictures for the funeral."

He turned with the box in hand and narrowed his eyes when he noticed Donna inside the house. "What?"

Elizabeth slipped in beside her, staying silent as instructed.

"We need photos we can put around the funeral parlor. It's traditional. Surely you remember?"

Cradling the box with one hand, he shot his right hand through his hair and sighed. "Maybe. So much to remember. I can barely believe this. Everything is such a blur. Let me put this down. What photos do you need?"

Just the opening she needed. "We'd need images of her life. Maybe some childhood photos, family photos, and wedding photos, of course."

The box rested on the table where Jeff placed it, and he moved toward an open living room area in the process. He stopped, stared at a couple of framed photos, and picked up one.

Before Donna could work up to what she *really* wanted to ask, Elizabeth spoke in a voice she must have assumed mimicked a

Southern accent, but sounded distorted, rather like a talking doll with low batteries, "Yee-all got some of your wife with her friends?"

The man stopped, clutching the framed photos to his chest, and then spun around. "Who are you?"

"Funeral home employee," Elizabeth offered in her weird voice.

Donna put her hand up to her mouth and whispered loudly, "Relative."

Nepotism, the practice of hiring unqualified friends and relatives over appropriate job applicants, still survived in the South. Jeff must have understood her message and nodded. "I think she has some photos in her bedroom."

They watched as Jeff disappeared down a hall. After a couple of minutes, with only the sound of classical music playing in the background, Elizabeth hissed, "Her bedroom. Did you hear that?"

"Not surprising." She held a finger to her lips when she heard footsteps coming back.

Jeff entered the room, his arms crammed with various framed photos. "Is this enough?"

"Perfect." She stepped forward to take the photos without looking at them. "Thanks. We'll be on our way."

Both women turned toward the entryway when a feminine voice carried down the hall. "Yoo-hoo! I saw the open door and let myself in."

"Not her again," Jeff groaned.

This sounded interesting, but to openly eavesdrop wouldn't work. Maybe their exit could be at a leisurely pace. She gave her fellow sleuth the side-eye, trying to communicate her thoughts. The message she received must have been to go in slow motion. Elizabeth lifted up a foot, leaving it suspended in the air, reminiscent of a child playing a game.

"Come on," Donna hissed as a middle-aged woman sporting a traditional short, ash blonde hairdo that supposedly hid the gray moved past them. Trying to notice as much as she could without being obvious, Donna settled for a nod of acknowledgment, which wasn't returned. Rude.

They made it to the door before Donna turned to stare at the woman who faced Jeff with her hands on her hips. She seemed familiar. Oh yeah, she saw her at the gardener meeting today.

Donna lingered at the door, not able to hear what the woman said, but Jeff yelled, "I don't know anything about your stupid hat or shears! Leave me alone!"

It sounded like they should hoof it out before they blocked the door when the complainer got thrown out. Still clutching the photos, Donna moved down the stairs with Elizabeth accompanying her. Once at the car, they stowed the photos in the trunk when a gunshot rang out. Donna grabbed Elizabeth's arm and pushed her down on the ground before joining her.

"What now?" Elizabeth queried in a high-pitched voice.

"We wait without talking. Could be the shooter won't notice us in a hurry to escape."

Donna squeezed her eyes shut, smelling the gardenias, and hoped this wouldn't be her last case. Even in the afterlife, she would still hear Mark say *let the professionals handle the dangerous stuff.* The problem was you never knew what qualified as risky until it was too late.

Chapter Seventeen

THE ROUGH SURFACE of the driveway bit into Donna's hands and face. From her position next to her car, she could peer under it and view the steps up to the veranda. In doing so, she couldn't help noticing how dirty the underneath of her car was. Geesh. Another thing she didn't want to be part of her exit. People would gossip that she had a dirty car, which would lead to talk about the inn and mention of the previous murders, and possibly the conclusion that the people weren't murdered but possibly died from food poisoning or another malady from unsanitary conditions. Rumors would circulate that Donna only made the murder story to throw people off the truth.

The thought forced a moan from her, which resulted in Elizabeth, lying beside her, to shoot an elbow into Donna's side, and then point wordlessly to a pair of large, green gardening boots tromping their way toward them. The wearer made no effort to be quiet. That certainty alone unnerved Donna. She pushed up on trembling arms and gritted her teeth, ready to face death on her terms. Maybe she could text the name of her killer to Mark, but only if she recognized the person and lived long enough to do so. Her dive to the ground sent her purse, along with her phone, skittering in the opposite direction. Stretching her arm as far as she could, her fingers failed to reach the strap.

Worst of all, she'd pulled Elizabeth into this deadly scenario. She was not a bad sort—opinionated and not great at following instructions—but the woman had moxie. No one deserved to die in a foreign country. It would be a nightmare for the relatives trying to get the body back home.

The best would be to evaluate the situation—fast. Her survey of her soon-to-be killer included a pair of chambray work pants, a little on the worn side. Large, wrinkled hands grasped an open shotgun. A navy and white logo-embellished shirt identified the man as an employee of Paradise Found Gardening Service along with his billed cap that covered shaggy, grey hair. Even though Donna knew folks in the area insisted on magazine-worthy yards and gardens, this man's reaction made no sense.

"We didn't step on the grass."

"I didn't think you did," the man holding the gun answered and then had the nerve to grin. "Came over because I thought the shooting might have alarmed the neighbors."

Elizabeth got back on her feet, brushed off her clothes, and addressed the man. "It's not like this all the time? Shooting and such?"

Another American stereotype she'd need to stomp out. Donna scrambled to her feet, curious to hear the man's explanation for shooting in an area where a woman had been found shot to death.

"Oh, no, ma'am," the man answered and shook his head. "Gophers. Nasty critters. Taking pot shots at rodents isn't my usual approach. With the garden tour coming up and all, Miss Emmeline is fit to be tied with those gophers ruining the lawn. They chewed through her waterline, shutting down the fountain with the pretty little mermaid in it. Mounds the size of a leatherback sea turtle dot the lawn. If that wasn't bad enough, they left dead spots in the yard from their underground snacking."

Before he could elaborate more, the demanding woman who had

forced their fast exit marched down the stairs. Seeing the man, she pointed to her right. "Otis, your work is over there, not jawing here."

The man touched two fingers to his cap. "Yes, Miss Emmeline." A short head bob acknowledged his departure, but Donna had to comment.

"She takes her gardening very seriously."

"Very," Otis answered before hurrying across the drive only to vanish into the hedges that divided the properties. Miss Emmeline followed and somehow managed to part the hedges in an angry fashion with much grabbing and grumbling.

Her heartbeat had slowed after she'd discovered that only rodents were in danger today. However, her would-be sleuth might be shaken to the core. Donna asked, "How are you?"

"Same as always." Elizabeth pressed a hand to her chest and gazed at the hedges where the two exited. "I'm gobsmacked with Miss Emmeline telling the gardener to shoot the gophers. They're just doing what gophers do."

Not certain what *gobsmacked* meant, Donna decided to rationalize it out. "You were surprised?"

"Yes, that's what I said." She shot Donna an odd look.

"Me, too. I was surprised that the garden owners didn't do their own gardening. Call me naïve. We'd better head on out."

The two of them climbed into the car. Air conditioning would cool them off and possibly blow off the sour smell of fear that still lingered on Donna. Nothing really happened, and the only critter in danger was a gopher, but why did she insist on doing this? Now she remembered. It made her pretty chuffed to put the clues together as fast as her husband did or faster. Wait. Did she just say *chuffed* in her mind? Before she knew it, she'd be calling everything bloody this and bloody that, which would embellish her reputation in a manner she chose not to dwell on.

Car on, air on, and the radio playing soothing classical music—everything she needed to bring down her blood pressure, except the music was angry sounding. Cannons even sounded. Donna clicked it off. "Okay. Ready for the next part of our mission?"

Elizabeth did a double take. "That wasn't it?"

"Oh, no," Donna assured, trying to hide a smile as she put the car into drive. "We go to the funeral home and drop off the photos. They need to be there for the funeral tomorrow."

"Makes sense." Elizabeth fastened her seatbelt and added, "Shouldn't we look at them?"

"Of course we look at them. We take photos of them first, and then we give them to the funeral home. Jeff will expect to see them tomorrow. Another rule in the sleuth book—when pretending to be a service person, do whatever task you said you would do."

"I'll keep that in mind."

"Never promise anything you can't do." That wasn't exactly true. Donna's motto centered on not promising anything if it could be traced back to you. Many things couldn't, especially if you never mentioned your name. "Good job not mentioning your name."

"I've done some fact-checking in my day," she uttered the words with a touch of smugness. "Won't we be recognized at the funeral?"

"I doubt it." Donna turned out of the long driveway and onto the road. "We'll wear hats. Many women will. Besides, no one will pay attention to us. They'll all come to scrutinize the grieving husband and try to decide if he looks like a murderer."

A small gasp came from the passenger side of the car. "Won't anyone be there for Margery?"

Afraid she'd painted the town as full of heartless gossips, Donna decided to try again. "Certainly. I'm sure Margery had many friends, and some of them will be speculating if Jeff is guilty. We'll need to look for the ones crying and those staring daggers at Jeff."

A few of the locals could cry on cue or at the drop of the hat. Mark complained the female portion of the town's known speeders were good sobbers. She added, "Maybe we should just look for the glarers."

"If a rival killed Margery, wouldn't she want Jeff to be guilty? If so, why should she glare at him?"

Another good point, but not one Donna would concede, just yet. "Southern women aren't normally killers, but when they are, they think it through. Sure, the murderer would glare at the husband to act just as upset as all the other friends."

"Brilliant," Elizabeth offered and tried to fist bump Donna, resulting in a hard swerve. "Oops."

"No problem," Donna said while righting the vehicle. "I didn't expect the fist bump."

"Don't they do that anymore?"

That was one Donna couldn't answer. "I have no clue. You'd have to ask someone under thirty."

This made them both laugh.

Chapter Eighteen

After delivering the photos to the funeral home, Donna headed home with Elizabeth, chattering about the experience. "What did you think about the funeral home? Posh. Everything was so fancy: opulent drapery, those cute little couches everywhere, and the flowers, tons of them."

"Not surprising about the flowers. With her being a member of the Gardening Club, I wouldn't be surprised if each member didn't try to outdo the other. It appears that Christmas came early for the florists. Aren't British funeral homes similar?"

"Some are, but different. Land is at a premium. Many funeral homes are found in former houses. It gives a bit of a homey feel. Others are like well-heeled gentlemen's clubs with leather chairs and hunting prints on the walls. Still others try to be all zen-like with fountains everywhere. What gets me is we waltz in and hand over the photos and no one acts daft about it."

"It's a small town. Legacy may be growing, but people trust each other. Besides, a funeral could involve the entire town. A popular saying mentions it takes a village to raise a child. Our version here is it takes a village to bury one."

"I get it."

Donna didn't know if she did or not, but she would eventually.

Surprisingly, things went quicker than she expected, which meant Donna would be home in time to fetch and carry for all the guests. Normally, she used the reception to find out more about the guests and if they were having a good time. It helped with her marketing to know the likes and dislikes of travelers. Right now, she needed downtime to think through what happened. Her mother and Thelma could handle the reception. There was a good chance Simon would come along to assist but would end up hobnobbing with the guests. At best, twelve guests would show at the buffet-style mixer. Many bypassed it, especially if they were on a romantic weekend.

"Want to try a Southern treat?"

"Certainly!"

As soon as the words took form, her mind raced madly, reaching for something close by that might be somewhat different from anything in jolly old England. It had to be something that didn't require reservations. Maybe even a little campy and selfie worthy. When it came to indulgent activities, her father had specialized in them. Every now and then, the two of them would sneak out to the Down-Home Diner. Besides being just a diner, it featured a gift shop with all the treats forbidden at their home, including Moon Pies and Goo Goo Clusters.

"I've got just the place. I need to check my phone to make sure it's open."

Donna signaled and then slid into two horizontal parking spaces. There was no need to park properly when she'd only be a few seconds. There was also no need to play with her phone while driving and end up with a ticket. Mark would never let her live it down. A little typing and some scrolling assured her not only was the Down-Home Diner still in business but it stayed open until nine, too. At last, something was going her way.

"Buckle up and get ready for some guilty pleasures," Donna announced with relish.

"I'm already buckled up."

"It's an expression."

Donna grinned, imagining she could already taste the fried pickles, cheese straws, and the deep-fried macaroni and cheese bites. Her mother labeled the place off-limits since she worried about her husband's health and her own waistline. Donna assumed for the longest time her mother never knew, but she did and had said nothing, allowing father and daughter to have a private indulgence.

After making the right amount of turns and passing sunburned tourists either returning to their lodgings or seeking out a popular eatery, a colorful building shaped like a lunch box complete with a metal handle at the top appeared, exactly where it should be. Outside the diner were large metal statues, including a giant rooster and a rocking coffee pot that continually tipped into a metal cup.

"Blimey!" Elizabeth said, straightening up and pivoting in her seat to observe everything. "It's a cross between a carnival and a food shop."

"That's a clever way of putting it."

They parked the car next to an SUV. Children erupted from the vehicle and posed by the metal flowers and glass mushrooms, waiting on their slow-moving parents to snap photos. So far, it was them and the picture-happy family. The place she remembered only had six booths and a few counter seats. "Let's go. Plenty of people walk here, and there's a limited number of seats inside."

The two of them hustled out of the car and into the mingled smells of pecan pie, fried okra, and the tang of pickles. Donna waved at the lone server and took one of the red booths, grabbing two laminated menus from behind the napkin dispenser. She handed one to Elizabeth.

"Take a gander."

Donna put up her hand and held up two fingers bringing the lone server their way with two frosty glass bottles of Coca-Cola and a bowl of salted peanuts.

After thanking the woman, Donna took a swig of icy soda and then stuffed peanuts down the neck of the bottle.

Elizabeth reacted as she'd expected. "What are you doing?"

"Try it. It's sweet and salty together. It's a Southern thing."

Even though her nose crinkled at the instructions, Elizabeth drank some of the liquid and then grabbed a handful of peanuts and stuffed them in the bottle. At the first sip, her eyebrows went up. "Not half bad."

"Yeah, I'd forgotten how good it was." She placed the bottle on the table. "We order and then we discuss what we've learned so far."

"Oooh," Elizabeth rubbed her hands together. "I like the sound of that." She tapped one finger on the menu. "What do you suggest? The High Cotton Platter, the Bless Your Heart, or the Cattywampus?"

"Definitely the Cattywampus. There are way too many goodies on the Bless Your Heart platter for one person. The High Cotton is too meat-heavy."

After giving their orders to a jovial server, they waited for a few moments before wiggling closer to speak.

Donna spoke. "The gunshot today scared me."

"Me, too. Thought I was a goner for a moment. Once the gardener showed up, it all made sense."

"Exactly." Donna took another swig of her sweet and salty concoction and folded her arms on the table. "Gophers aren't all that easy to get rid of. More likely there's now a colony. I suspect they didn't find their way into that garden just in time for the garden tours."

"Possibly. Would shooting be the natural result of the infestation?"

"Not really. Most would use a mixture of castor oil and soap. Still, it takes time, which explains the shooting."

"A gunshot is loud. It rattled my brain."

"Not too surprising," she commented while trying to search her memory for how loud a shotgun blast really was. Mark compared it to louder than a rock concert, but that might depend on what type of concert you went to. "An average gunshot is louder than a jackhammer or an ambulance. It makes me wonder if the gardener is trying to shoot the gophers or just annoy them into moving."

The server carried two steaming platters to their booth. "Eat up, y'all."

"We will," Elizabeth announced, bringing about a wide smile from their server. The diner's door-mounted bell jingled, admitting the picture happy family. They sent their server to address her newest customers while Donna pondered Margery's neighbors' reaction or lack of one.

"Maybe no one was home, but a gunshot in the neighborhood went unnoticed by anyone but us."

"You'd think someone would have called the police, certain someone was being murdered, but truth be told, there's plenty of folks shooting off their guns, usually just target practice. I guess we all kind of assumed no one is murdering one another, even though this has been proven otherwise."

"Do you think most would ignore gunshots?" Elizabeth bit into a cheese straw. "These are super."

Donna used her index finger to shape her eyebrow as she spoke. "No, but if people knew the gardener was shooting at gophers, they wouldn't be too alarmed."

On that note, she agreed with a nod and bit into her fried bologna and tomato sandwich, chewed thoughtfully, and then swallowed. "Why would the gardener come over and announce to us what he was doing?"

About to cut into her fried green tomato, Elizabeth froze. "Right." She finished cutting her tomato, bit into it, and closed her eyes. "Mmmm, delicious. How long has the husband been back?"

"Barely a day. He was gone when his wife was murdered, although she lay in the garden practically twenty-four hours. Makes sense the husband wouldn't know Otis was gunning for gophers. Probably should have notified him before he started shooting."

"Common courtesy for a man who just had his wife shot in the back garden." Elizabeth managed to point with her pinkie to the apple butter while gripping a fried biscuit.

Donna gave the glass container a little push to put it within reach. "Sounds about right. What's more peculiar was why wasn't she discovered before then? All the houses in that area have a primo view of the ocean, and most have terraced stairs to walk to the ocean. I do the garden tour every year, and I noticed every house has a back balcony or veranda coming off the second or third floor. The height allows guests to be a little jealous of the view, while allowing the occupants a good view of their neighbors' doings."

Elizabeth managed a surprised arch of the brows since her mouth remained full.

It was understandable since the poor dear had probably never tasted any of the fried delicacies before. Donna chose to continue explaining, "Yeah, I'm guilty of gazing at the gardens of the rich. The money from the garden tours ticket sales goes to our local literacy chapter, which buys books for children and puts them in free corner libraries. That's my rationale for going every year."

Elizabeth swallowed hard and reached for her bottle of soda only to find it empty. Before she could say anything, the server appeared with two icy bottles. "I saw y'all were running low."

They both thanked the server and assured her they were enjoying their meal. The father of the photo clan whistled and snapped his fingers, drawing a murmured retort from the server. "Tourist." She reddened and pressed her hand to her chest, and then spoke to Elizabeth. "I didn't mean you."

"I know. Better see to your tourist and his tribe." She reached for her soda and drank while Donna continued explaining.

"There are no fences between the yards. It has something to do with the HOA or something. People can plant trees, hedges, flower beds, etc. You'd think someone would see a dead woman in the yard, especially the nearest neighbor, who's so worried about her lawn that her gardener is shooting gophers or at least attempting to."

Waving a cheese straw, Elizabeth said, "It makes you wonder about Miss Emmeline."

"That, I am. We need to see the crime photos to see exactly where Margery fell when shot. That could tell us a great deal if she were visible from next door. That means we need to finish up."

"I'll hurry," Elizabeth stated, cramming the rest of the cheese straw into her mouth.

Donna held the flat of her palm out as if stopping traffic. "Slow down, honey. When I said we needed to finish up, I meant in about fifteen or twenty minutes. We haven't even hit the gift store yet. You'll want to pick up some Moon Pies for Howard or even a Cheerwine drink. An excess of sugar brightens anyone's day. Don't forget to remind him to brush."

Chapter Nineteen

THE SUMMER MOON sank low on the horizon, leaving streaks of red and violet in its wake. It was not quite night, but close to it, adding to the relaxed quality of the atmosphere. Donna opened her car door and hoped all the dishes were cleared up. She'd still need to prep for breakfast, but she'd put on a pot of coffee and discuss the case with her hubby as she worked.

Her lips twisted as Elizabeth shut the car door. There were no complaints about the amount of pressure she used to close the door, but having the two Brits in the mix might change her evening plans. Occasionally, she joked about folks being so set in their ways they couldn't try new things. A few of her guests were like that even to the point of bringing their own sheets and their own cereal so their bed and breakfast could be just like home. It made her wonder why they even bothered to travel.

Mercy. She never wanted to think of herself as being that inflexible. She waved at guests heading to their cars. "Have a nice evening."

Even though she had no investment in the guests, Elizabeth waved, too. Her upbeat personality and gung-ho attitude helped Donna decide what she needed to do next.

"I imagine you want to get showered and visit with your husband."

"It's a possibility," she acknowledged with a shrug, then smirked. "Depends if there's something better on the radar."

"Might be." Donna surveyed the parking lot for the oversized luxury coupe that Simon and Cecilia used. Spotting it, she wrinkled her nose. Her mother would love to chit-chat with her British guests. On the upside, she had the current gossip from the gardening meeting.

"I have to prep for breakfast, but I'll put on a pot of decaf while Mark and I analyze the case." A wistful expression brightened her countenance. "We used to do this before we married. That's how I knew he was serious."

A heartfelt sigh sounded, and Elizabeth said, "It sounds romantic."

"How a person died, killer motivations, the identity of the murderer, and possible suspects aren't the sweet nothings most women want to hear."

"Not the crime, but the sharing. I'd love to be a fly on the wall as you discuss. It might inspire my Howie."

Never having been one to inspire envy, Donna found herself pushing back her shoulders and lifting her chin. She liked the feeling her marriage had something Elizabeth wanted in her own. Call it pride, but she could be big enough to role model for the other couple. "Sure. If you feel up to it after today."

"Woo-hoo!" Elizabeth rocked up to her tiptoes, then bounced. "I'm buzzing."

"That's the sugar," Donna inhaled audibly. "I should have warned you. Most Southern treats use a heavy hand with the sugar if they're not deep-fried. Sometimes, they still do even if they are, such as beignets."

"Oh no! I meant I was over the moon." Laughter escaped her lips as she shook her head. "I can't wait. We'll have a whale of a time."

Donna locked the car, contemplating the *whale of the time*

comment. Hopefully, no one would get harpooned. "Let's go see if everything is cleaned up."

They entered through the back door only to hear voices coming from the kitchen. Donna hesitated for a moment. Maybe they didn't get things cleaned up in a timely fashion. In that case, she'd be stuck with the dishes. Before she could contemplate using the front door, Jasper let out a warning bark. Burglars could sneak through the house and past the sleeping pooch, but let her put one foot in the house and the dog reacted like an alarm system.

She might as well see what needed to be done. Donna managed an amiable mien as she entered the kitchen. Mark, Howard, Simon, and Cecilia gathered around the island, chatting. Her mother gave a finger wave.

Mark slid off the stool and kissed her on the cheek. "Did you deliver your condolence food?"

"I did," she answered, with as little elaboration as possible.

Mark knew she snooped and probably had given up on stopping her from doing so. All the same for the benefit of his blood pressure, she chose tidbits of her activities to divulge at a time. Some never entered into the discussion.

Howard greeted his wife with a wide smile. "How's my favorite girl? Any American events today?"

That's all it took. Elizabeth's eyes lit up, and she entered, talking. "Oh my, yes! We visited a suspected murderer and gathered photos of the victim as a ruse since Thelma had said rival. Then someone shot at us, we stopped at a posh funeral home, and then hid at the Down-Home Diner, discussing the case until the dishes were done."

Cecilia leveled a censorious look on Donna, but it was hard to know if it was for skipping out on the cleaning or visiting the sugar palace. Surely her mother had to be over her dislike of the place by now.

Howard, in a delayed reaction, jumped up and shouted. "Shot at?"

"Not shot at," Donna felt the need to clarify before the top of Howard's head flew off like in cartoons. Apparently, Elizabeth needed to learn the importance of delivering things in little bites. "We heard gunshots. The shooter was a gardener shooting at gophers." She delivered the words in a matter-of-fact fashion. "That's all."

She walked over to the coffee pot and sniffed. Not fresh, but not old, either. It would do. The coffee splashed into her cup as Simon spoke.

"The garden tour date is coming up fast. Still, shooting at a gopher smacks of desperation. Good chance of messing up the yard even more."

"True," Mark agreed and picked up his coffee cup.

Howard scratched at his brow, and he may have paled a tad, but it was hard to be sure. His eyes traveled from speaker to speaker rather like a tennis match watcher. "Shooting at gophers? My wife was in danger."

"Ha!" Elizabeth forced a laugh and landed a playful punch on my husband's arm. "I wasn't afraid. Besides, I just said that to see if you were listening. I'm ready to talk about the clues we've gathered."

That shut up the outraged Scotland Yard Detective Inspector in a hurry. He gestured to his stool, which his wife took. There were more stools in the pantry, and Mark went to snag two.

Donna put her cup on the island and then knelt to fondle her dog. "How's my good boy?"

His spritely tail wag served as a reply.

By the time Mark returned with the chairs, her mother was holding court on possible motivations. "There's always the gal on the side."

A derisive snort sounded and Donna declared, "He always *had* a gal on the side. I heard he had three."

"Of course you did." Her mother nodded and took on the air of knowing something no one else did.

"What? You know something? It's your duty to tell."

Cecilia remained smug and silent until Mark cleared his throat and told her, "If it's pertinent to the case, you should tell."

A few more seconds passed before Cecilia said, "Oh, okay." She glanced in Donna's direction. "I wanted to hold out longer since you not only stuck me with clean up, but you also failed to bring me anything from the Down-Home Diner."

While Elizabeth purchased her own treats, Donna had bought rock candy as a nostalgic treat for Mark and herself, but she'd give up her prize to move the brainstorming along. "How do you know I didn't?"

Opening her purse, she located the small bag from the diner. She handed it to her mother, who opened it and grinned. "Rock candy! I haven't seen that in years."

"Three women?" Donna prompted, afraid her mother might go down the candy memory lane.

"Margery started that rumor."

"Why?" Donna questioned and gazed around the room at the others to see if they were as surprised as her. Simon played with his coffee spoon as if the story had been heard one too many times. "Why would she want her husband to look bad?"

"No pre-nup, or it could be the pre-nup was too generous. I'm not sure. What I do know is Jeff is a vain man as well as being a flirt. It wouldn't take much for people to believe the gossip."

The conversation caused Mark to reach for his ever-present pocket tablet and pen. He hovered the pen over the pad and asked, "Was she planning to divorce him?"

"Possibly. She kept mum on that matter. Theirs was an odd marriage—not exactly a love match, and she held the purse strings. I always thought they married for companionship, yet they never did things together. She'd been dropping hints about philandering before. Even naming names of women who…" She stretched out the last word in a wheedling tone. "…might be open to such an arrangement."

This explanation took more twists and turns than a roller coaster. Donna held up her hand. "All right, are you saying all the stories about his affairs are fake?"

"The stories Margery spun are. All the same, our boy has been seen in the company of a woman other than his wife in other cities. It could be if his wife chose to brand him as a rake, he might as well live up to the part. Even Casanovas fall in love. He may have decided it was time to move on with his gal pal."

"Murder is so extreme," Elizabeth protested, upset at the prospect or possibly for the victim.

"It's profitable, too," Donna couldn't help pointing out.

Cecilia steepled her fingers thoughtfully. "I'm going with Jeff as the guilty party." She held up one finger. "He decides he's found his soulmate." The second finger joined the first. "He stands to get insurance money and everything else. With a divorce, he loses at least half, maybe more."

Her mother excelled in gossip and digging through it for a nugget of truth, but she may have missed some nuggets. "If Margery was bad-mouthing her own husband and had done this for a while, would she be leaving him much in the will? It could turn out that everything went to the Master Gardener's Educational Fund. It would be an excellent way to stick it to a murderous spouse."

"All good points," Mark said and rubbed his large palm over his face. "I wish it were that easy. The man has an airtight alibi. At the time the medical examiner affixed the time of death, Dr. Jeff was waxing poetic on how untreated gum disease can spread to the brain. While I don't find it the most stimulating subject, his ever-helpful assistant recorded it and put it up online."

"Those time dates on the video can be faked," Howard inserted. "We've been fooled more than once with that."

"I don't doubt that." Mark's hand went to the back of his neck, affirming what kind of a day it had been. "Plenty of people attended that talk. It's more than time stamped. What we have is a husband with an alibi, but he could have hired someone else."

"Ah yes," Howard smiled at all of them as he warmed up to his tale. "It reminds me of a case I once had."

Donna forced herself to stare at the pass-through door so she wouldn't be guilty of rolling her eyes. Everything reminded him of an important case he'd somehow solved on his own. However, he didn't make detective by twiddling his thumbs, which meant she should listen.

"It's one of the oldest tales in the book. Two men who meet don't know each other that well. They start drinking and tell each other their marital woes. First, they joke about killing their wives and then decide they need an alibi—something where they were too far away for them to be the murderer. They shake hands. No money is exchanged. No emails. Just an address or a photo and a promise. I imagine they have to settle on times to make it work. They simply kill each other's wives. If they're lucky, they don't get caught."

"Ahem!" Simon cleared this throat. "Should we assume the man was caught if you're telling us the tale?"

"Correct." Howard tilted up his chin and crossed his arms. "Bloody fools. Ordinary folks aren't cold-blooded killers, at least not all of them. The second guy choked when his wife was blown away. Ended up confessing as opposed to completing his part of the deal."

Fingernails drummed on the island as each person contemplated if the tale could have any applications to the current situation. "Well." Mark shot a hand through his hair that needed a trim. "We need to figure out if another wife is in danger."

It wasn't the opening she wanted, but darn it, no one mentioned the obvious, probably because they hadn't thought of it yet. "When we dropped by Jeff's, I watched both the gardener and Emmeline cross into their own yard. I realized how close the yards are and how the HOA prohibited fences. With Emmeline and her gardener working to get the garden ready, wouldn't they notice a dead woman next door?"

"Good point." Mark reached over to pat Donna's shoulder. "Did my favorite sleuth come up with anything else today?"

Before Donna could ask for the crime scene photos to prove her theory, her junior sleuth Elizabeth spoke in a rush, her words stumbling over each other. "The gardener running around shooting at gophers would hide the actual gunshot. Maybe the gophers weren't a natural occurrence."

"Brilliant," Howard remarked, then puffed out his chest. "Who knew my love had such sharp deductive skills?"

Not to mention *stealing credit*, though Donna chose not to mention it. Instead, her sharp mind kept working, turning over possibilities, until she found one. "What if the gophers were a gift, not from the killer, but from a gardening rival. As for the gardener shooting at the gophers, the killer could use this as a chance-met opportunity, or he or she may have used a silencer."

"Good call," Mark commented, "So far, we have the husband as a suspect or someone he might have hired."

Elizabeth leaned forward on her stool and waved in Mark's direction. "Don't forget the rival. Thelma mentioned a rival."

Speaking of which, Donna glanced around. Her resident psychic hadn't attended this confab. "By the way, where *is* Thelma?"

Her mother pursed her lips and tutted. "You'd think you'd know more about your own staff. She's recording her podcast, *The Psychic's in the House.* She does it every week. I can't wait for this week's episode: 'Hearing Voices from Beyond.'"

"Oh yeah, that," Donna answered. She inhaled heavily, irritated her mother knew more about what went down on this planet than she did. "Yeah, I can't wait for it, either."

Chapter Twenty

"I T's ALWAYS MONEY!" Howard concluded, hitting the island top with his fisted hand. Howard, Elizabeth, Mark, and Donna were still gathered in the kitchen, debating the most recent murder. The kitschy cat clock's tail and eyes moved side to side. Donna suspected the cat might be as bored as she was. Cecilia and Simon slipped out with the excuse of an early bedtime. Donna knew her mother tended to be a night owl.

The money angle took center stage for the last hour or more. Inheritance, insurance, or selling off the assets and estate would provide plenty of money.

Her mother's gossip connections failed her, but surprisingly, Simon played golf regularly with the top life insurance guys. Fortunately, he had a game scheduled the next day—yet another excuse for them to leave. As a former Asheville resident, he wouldn't be expected at the funeral. As for his golfing buddies, their wives would represent them.

Feeling mischievous, Donna caught her husband's eye and asked, "What if it isn't money?"

A choking sound came from Howard as his eyes bulged. Jumping into action, Mark thumped him on the back. "You okay, buddy?"

He sputtered and shook off Mark's hand. "I'm fine. Coffee must have gone down the wrong way."

Only, he hadn't been drinking any. Apparently, no one ever bothered to disagree with the Scotland Yard Detective Inspector until then, and she wasn't done by a long shot. "What if Jeff had a gal on the side who was getting tired of waiting?"

Plenty of mistresses eventually grew weary of the someday promise and set an ultimatum, forcing their non-committal boyfriend into some sort of action. Usually, it didn't turn out to be the action they wanted. Even when they thought they'd won, all they really had was a man who'd cheat on his wife.

"We haven't established Jeff has a girlfriend." Howard lifted his chin, adding to his already superior air. No wonder Elizabeth never got to contribute much. "Cecilia mentioned that Margery made up the rumors."

Please. Could the man be a detective and know so little about human nature? Maybe it was Americans he didn't understand, and everything *was* about money in England. All the same, he might benefit from learning a thing or two.

"Rumors are like smoke. There is a reason for them. Jeff is a flirt, which is well known. It feeds his vanity. Most men engage in affairs to prove they're attractive and still have it. He has no reason not to because most people think he already is."

Howard sniffed, making clear his opinion. "We should wait to see if a large insurance policy was written recently for Margery Baumgarten."

"We can do that," Donna agreed. "However, it wouldn't have to be recent. I imagine an old money person like herself would already have a sizable insurance policy. The real question is who benefits from it. Most insurance companies won't pay out on a murder since a criminal can't benefit from the crime. The company will hold payment until the murder is solved or at least until the beneficiaries aren't under suspicion."

Elizabeth teetered on her stool, almost asleep, and then jerked. "We might be gone by then!"

"We'll do our best to solve it before then," Mark promised with a wide grin. "I think we should all get to bed. The funeral is at ten. I need to get my plain clothes people into place."

"Really?" Donna inquired with a lifted brow. "Everyone in Legacy knows everyone else."

"That's why it will work. Delaney is related to the Baumgarten family. Lopez's mother used to cook for Margery's parents. A few others could show up because everyone is there. Funerals are big in Legacy. Most people are invited, and those who aren't often crash."

During mid-yawn, Elizabeth spoke as she slid off the stool. "People crash funerals?"

"Oh yeah," Donna acknowledged but tried to suppress a chuckle and failed. "The last funeral I attended, the man's ex showed up, which surprised everyone since they didn't part on good terms. Still, no one thought much of it, thinking she came to make her final farewells, until the minister asked if anyone would like to say a few words. She marched up there and reminded everyone that her ex, Billy Joseph, got caught more than once taking more than his share of deer during hunting season, called in sick at the concrete plant when he was just hungover, which was about once a week, and he always managed to weasel out of paying his portion of the bar tab."

"What a sod!" Howard exclaimed, grimacing a bit. "What about not speaking ill of the dead? Didn't anyone stop her?"

"Well, she wasn't throwing anything or cussing. Besides, Billy Joseph *did* run around on her. Maybe most felt she needed to have her say. Now, if she continued to badmouth her dead former husband months later, that would be bad manners."

It was close to eleven and Donna hadn't finished prepping for breakfast. As a hint, she ambled to the sub-zero fridge and started pulling out fruit for the citrus salad. She called over her shoulder. "Mark, can you get a box of Danishes from the downstairs freezer? Bring me up some of the gluten-free bread, too."

"Got it," Mark answered as he strolled to the basement door.

"That sounds like our cue to leave," Howard announced in a fake hearty tone.

Hopefully, he didn't use that one on the suspects. Too obvious. Donna put the cutting board and a chef's knife on the island and went to the sink to wash her hands.

Elizabeth used her hand in a shooing motion. "Go on, Howie. I'll be up in a second."

As the husband in question headed upstairs, Elizabeth sidled up to Donna and whispered, "I needed to get him out of the way. He thinks everyone is motivated by money. I'll admit many criminals are, but sometimes it's a crime of passion. That's why we need to follow Jeff and find out who's his lady love. He may not have killed her, but a woman determined to become the next missus would have sufficient motivation."

Donna managed a head bob, thinking the dubious honor of marrying Jeff should not be sufficient motivation for anyone. "Uh-huh. Good chance we'll see her at the funeral. Not to attend would be noticed."

"Good call." She popped one thumb up before she disappeared behind the interior door, just as Mark entered the kitchen carrying frost-tinged packages.

"Anything I should know?" He angled his head in the direction Elizabeth went.

"Not much. She wants to tail Jeff and find out who the girlfriend is. Believes the girlfriend could have done it."

"Interesting." Mark placed his burdens on the island and rubbed his hands together to warm them. "Big mistake not listening to his wife. After all, a woman knows better how a woman might think. What's your opinion?"

"It *could* happen. Wouldn't be the first time a girlfriend wiped out the competition." Donna's eyes rolled upward as she tried to remember details of a celebrity case. "A few of the impatient females take it upon themselves, never mentioning it to their man, which is unfortunate for all because they'd probably find out their guy never wanted to change things."

She picked up the knife and sectioned the oranges, releasing the strong, vibrant scent into the kitchen. After cutting for a minute or so, she pointed her knife at Mark. "I'd better not hear about you running around on me. I'd have to deal with your crazy girlfriend trying to murder me."

Mark chuckled, moved behind his wife, and nuzzled her neck. "I'm no idiot. You're the best thing to ever happen to me."

A warmth blossomed inside of Donna. She may not have thought of her husband as a silver-tongued devil when they first met, but he certainly improved with time. Sometimes, he'd say something so sweet she'd melt.

"Uh-huh. Go on."

Mark placed a kiss on the nape of her neck before stepping back. "Only a fool angers a woman who knows her way around knives the way you do."

He went and ruined the warm feeling by saying something he thought was funny but wasn't. Two could play that game. "Don't ever forget it."

Chapter Twenty-One

MORNING CAME WAY too early with Mark's phone buzzing. In the early dawn light, her husband blinked, his voice still rough from sleep as he answered. "Taber here."

An indecipherable mumble sounded to which Mark responded. "Not a big deal. It's okay if you don't wear a suit. It's summer and ninety degrees. No one would expect it. Most of the other men will show up in dress shirts and khakis. A few would push the limit with shorts. Don't do that. That would draw attention and censure."

Funeral, Donna reminded herself. One more thing on her ever-increasing to-do list along with reminding her husband about the photos. She stretched, waiting for her husband to end the call, and then rolled over and poked him. "Photos."

He faced her with a lazy smile. "Good morning to you, too."

Donna pushed up into a seated position. "Good morning. You know what I mean. Maybe you didn't want to talk about the photos in front of Howard."

A hearty exhale greeted her comment. "Wow! You're right. Super sleuth strikes again." He sat up, put his feet on the floor, and wiggled his shoulders briefly to shake out the stiffness. "I've tried to tell Howard how much help you are to me. Since the director kept hovering around, I didn't get to say too much. You know how he is about you."

That, she did. Donna pressed her lips together and narrowed her eyes as if seeing the officious man in her room. Whenever anyone mentioned her helping on a previous case, he made an ugly face to express his distaste. "That useless paper pusher has no use for women helping on cases."

Thinking of the way the man belittled her assistance had her grinding her teeth. As far as she could tell, all he did was cause chaos in the department. In truth, he was more of a micro-managing chief, who chose to call himself *commissioner* since it sounded much grander.

Her husband excelled at calming down people pulled over for traffic violations as well as those few victims of violent crime. "Now, Donna," he started, using his slow, low, calming voice. "The commissioner isn't against women."

Not buying it, she gave a derisive sniff. "Can't prove it by me. I bet you didn't tell him I'm lending a hand."

Mark yawned and rubbed the back of his neck. "You know I didn't. Civilians aren't supposed to know about the case." He snorted. "Yeah, try to keep the locals from gossiping about it. We can't do much about that. All I know is I'm pretty close to retirement, and I'd like to keep my pension. A few despicable officials in neighboring counties let veteran officers go right before retirement to save money. That's never happened here, but there could be a first time. I don't want it to be me."

"Geesh. I had no clue. Never liked him, not even for a second. You should have his job. Everyone thinks so."

A heavy sigh escaped Mark, and he shot a hand through his already mussed, thick, salt and pepper hair, rumpling it even more. "You know I don't want the job. I wouldn't have time to pour wine at the receptions."

His appearance at the receptions serving as a wine steward could be spotty even without the commissioner position. Thankfully, her family members stepped in when needed. However, she didn't point it out. "You're right. I'm glad to have you around instead of working long hours at the station."

"Yeah, I saw what you did there." He gave her an exaggerated wink. "Figured you'd mention the times I didn't show up for my wine steward and sometime bouncer job. For that, I have a surprise for you."

This was exciting. Her husband came up with the best gifts. She interlaced her fingers and bounced on the bed. "I can't wait."

"Don't get too excited. It's not that kind of present." He turned, pulled open the drawer of his bedstand, and withdrew a manila envelope. "I had the crime photographer make doubles. Told him I needed to study them at home."

It was the crime photos he didn't want to talk about last night. He had them all along. Donna lunged across the bed, grabbed the envelope, and opened it. "You were weird last night when I asked you about the photos."

"Yeah, I know."

Donna shook out the glossy photos that were in both color and black and white. Odd details pop out with the use of black and white photography. The slight shift of her husband's voice piqued her attention. "Howard? You chose not to say anything in front of him?"

"You read me so well. He's another who thinks only licensed professionals can help on a case."

A grunt answered his comment since Donna suspected as much due to Elizabeth's comments. Rather than address the remark, she focused on the photos. The first color photo showed an expansive garden with a rolling lawn, graceful trees, and classical goddess statues anchoring the lush flower gardens. Her eyes traveled over the photo, admiring the garden but looking for the body.

"Garden looks great. Margery would have been in the running for bragging rights this year. A shame she missed out on winning."

"There's talk about Jeff allowing the house to stay on the tour."

Donna stayed quiet, having located the body by the water feature. Margery fell forward; a wide-brimmed straw hat hid her head. This photo had been taken from a distance. There had to be closer ones. She spread the photos across the sheets. A close-up showed a pair of garden shears and a basket of dead-headed blooms lying next to Margery. Someone took out the poor dear while she tidied her garden. A pang squeezed her heart as she thought about the woman she hadn't known well. At least she died doing what she loved.

Her finger tapped on the photo. "She's by the water lily pond. You said she was found in the lilies."

Mark stepped closer and stared down at the photos. "Yeah, she's in the lilies."

While Donna knew she didn't qualify as a master gardener, even she knew the difference between a stargazer lily and a water lily. The stargazers had bloomed out weeks ago. "Water lilies. It makes sense. Maybe she has koi fish. Perhaps she stopped to admire them. Then out of nowhere, a bullet took her out."

"That sounds about right."

She moved the photos around, trying to get a view from Miss Emmeline's house. "I've been on the tour before. I know the acreage on the left belongs to an absentee owner who's planning to build but hasn't yet. The property ends at a cliff. Emmeline's yard is on the right. You'd think the killer could have pushed her off the cliff. It would look like an accident or a suicide. Why not go that way?"

"Good point, as usual." Mark moved to the dresser, removed some clothes, and then headed to the bathroom. Before he entered, he threw out, "Could be someone Margery feared. She'd be on her guard if this person were nearby. A high-powered rifle with a scope could be shot from a distance with a decent marksman."

The bathroom door closed, leaving Donna with even more questions. Who would Margery be afraid of? Expertise with firearms could be almost anyone. It would be easier to find someone without any gun skills. The close-up of Margery with her right hand outstretched made Donna wonder if she'd seen her killer, perhaps even waved before being shot. Waving at strangers happened to be part of Southern hospitality tradition Then again, she could have seen someone she knew—someone who wouldn't be out of place in the yard next door.

The aroma of coffee drifting under the door pulled her out of the funk she'd fallen into while thinking of a friendly Margery possibly waving to her killer. "Margery, I *will* find your killer. I could use some hints though, or maybe a glowing neon arrow pointing to the guilty party."

She waited.

Nothing.

Not that she expected anything. Still, she had a resident psychic currently brewing coffee. Maybe she had something besides the word *rival* to help out with the case.

Chapter Twenty-Two

THE INN'S KITCHEN bustled as Thelma grabbed the warm cinnamon buns and carried them to the dining room. Donna plated the frittata. Instead of hanging out in the dining room like the other guests, Elizabeth perched on a stool. Tearing off pieces of buttered toast and feeding them to an appreciative Jasper, she threw out questions to a busy Donna.

"Have you studied the photos yet?"

Thinking she meant the crime scene photos, Donna lifted a filled tray and answered. "I did. No fences as I remembered, but it's hard to know where one yard ends and another begins."

As she delivered the entrées to the dining room, she puzzled over the confused expression on Elizabeth's face. Each guest received a wide smile as her mind turned over the confused mien of the would-be sleuth. *Wait.* Elizabeth hadn't seen the crime photos. She must have meant the photos they delivered to the home.

Back in the kitchen, Elizabeth progressed from toast to feeding Jasper bacon, earning a furry friend for life. While the old puggle was open to all human food treats, with the exception of vegetables, they didn't always agree with him.

Donna cleared her throat, hoping to end the feeding by distraction. "Ah, the funeral photos. Nope, I haven't studied them."

"What?" Her brows knitted, and she laid the rest of the bacon on the island. "Why did you say you did?"

"Not good at multi-tasking." She pulled the veggie links out of the microwave and put them on a bread plate for her vegan guest. "I thought you meant the crime scene photos."

The open-mouthed gape amused Donna as she backed out to deliver the soy sausages. There would be questions when she returned. Maybe she could bribe her into helping clean the kitchen by promising a peek at the crime scene photos. The assistance would give her a little more time to get ready for the funeral.

Howard and Mark chose to eat their breakfast in the dining room while Elizabeth passed on breakfast since she had nibbled her way through the preparation. Both Donna and Thelma nibbled on the leftover frittata and citrus salad.

Thelma mentioned between bites, "We need to fill up the snack pantries. They're pretty low." Using her fork as a pointer, she directed it at both Donna and Elizabeth. "You both were in my dream last night."

In the past two months, Thelma gave various cryptic pro-nouncements that either made no sense or hinted at bad things yet to come. Never did she mention winning lottery numbers or even happy surprises.

All the same, politeness demanded she inquire about the nature of the dream. "What was the dream like?"

"Odd." Thelma cocked her head, stared off at a blank spot on the wall, and then continued eating.

"That's it?" Donna couldn't believe the woman who threw out predictions like a parade clown throwing candy had gone peculiarly silent. She gestured with a hand for her to continue. "You know you can't say something like that and then stop."

"Stage presence." Thelma turned slowly and smiled. "I'm work-ing on it for my podcast and eventual live shows."

"The dream?" Elizabeth prompted. With her elbows on the island, she leaned toward Thelma. "I don't think I've had anyone dream about me before. Makes me feel somewhat important. I'd love to hear about your dream."

"Okay," Thelma agreed. She shot Donna a look that basically announced that's how you ask. "Keep in mind, as a psychic, even when I'm asleep, my gift is manifesting itself. In the dream, I could hear the ocean, the two of you were walking, and there was a cloud coming toward you. Danger! Danger was headed your way. Then I woke up."

Living in a coastal town, the roar of the ocean could be heard almost everywhere as long as no annoying car with oversized speakers idled nearby. "A cloud? You didn't see anything else? Should we be worried about a pop-up storm?"

Thelma shrugged. "It's a gift and a feeling. What it isn't is a reality show. Those things are researched. It ruins it for the rest of us. People assume actual psychics have some lackeys searching online for pertinent information." She snorted. "Besides, I don't approach strangers and give readings."

Her injured act pulled a derisive snort from Donna. "As I recall, when we first met, you said something about a disturbance in the atmosphere and murder."

"Oh, that." Thelma pulled on her ear and shrugged. "Not the same. I needed help from you. Not a reading, but a plea for assistance."

Elizabeth's eyes grew large and then she asked, "Is there anything else we should know about the current murder?"

"Be aware of your surroundings. Don't take your safety for granted. Stay alert. Danger abounds."

Elizabeth managed a serious head bob and added, "That's the

exact same thing my mum said when I told her we were going to America."

How weird was that? Donna crinkled her nose. "Danger abounds? Your mother actually said that?"

"No, not that. She told me to hold onto my purse. I settled on one of those cross the body bags. It's about the same thing."

"Not really." There was no need to point out losing your wallet wasn't the same as losing your life. "Let's get the place tidied up and then we can stare at the pictures and see if anything comes to us."

TWENTY MINUTES LATER, the dishwasher hissed, and the clary sage scent of the kitchen cleaner hung in the air. Donna took a tea towel and dried the island top to make sure no wetness remained to mar the photos. She decided to review the cell phone shots she took of the pictures she'd managed to gather for the funeral and pulled her phone from her pocket.

A young Margery stood with her arm around the family dog. Both stared at the camera with amused expressions as if they shared a secret. Just as well. The young Margery had no clue of her violent end at the time. Donna showed the picture to Elizabeth, who made a sympathetic sigh.

Elizabeth pressed a hand to her heart. "How sweet."

Donna pulled up another photo as a slightly chubby teenage Margery in a striped two-piece struck a sultry pose. There was nothing to be had from that image. The next one featured a sunburned Jeff and Margery with a cruise ship in the background. Surprisingly, they looked happy. She passed her phone to both Elizabeth and Thelma.

Thelma indicated the phone. "Anyone seeing this photo would think they were in love."

"Could be they were." Donna held out her hand for the phone. "It must have been their honeymoon before they really got to know one another." She caught the eyes of both women as she took her phone. "You know how people are when they're dating. Best manners, both well groomed, and the woman gets to pick the movie and restaurant. Your guy watches rom coms with you and pretends to like it. He might even go..." Donna paused for emphasis on the next word. "...*shopping* with you."

All three of the women chuckled, and Elizabeth commented with a fond smile, "My Howie used to take me to champagne brunch at one of the posh hotels." Her smile slipped as she continued. "Not anymore. He calls it a pretentious show and a waste of money. I guess that shows we are truly married that we can be so honest."

"Ha!" Thelma forced the bark of laughter. "Men might call it honesty, but plenty of wives keep their lips sealed, not wanting to rock the boat."

"Probably," Donna remarked, not wanting to get into a side discussion and returned to her phone, scrolling until she came to the next picture. A bunch of middle-aged ladies crowded together, displaying their hands clad in floral gardening gloves. "Must be the gardening group."

"Let me see," Elizabeth said, leaning into Donna to peer at the image. "They all look alike."

"Oh," Donna hadn't even considered this. Most of the women in the photo were either her age or older. Almost all had ash-blonde streaked hair to hide the gray, and pale skin, except for Doris, who did her best to emulate Malibu Barbie. "I see what you mean."

"Rivals." Thelma spoke in an ominous tone.

It was the same word her psychic helper had used before. Saying it again didn't make things any clearer. "Could you give me a specific name? How about pointing to one of the women?"

Leaning closer, she narrowed her eyes and hummed a little under her breath for a few seconds. "Nope. As I say, it's a gift. It doesn't work like the person who hands you the name of Miss America. I've got to go anyhow. Got an appointment."

"You'll miss the funeral."

Thelma replied, "You can represent the both of us."

"Okay, I will." Donna waved and then went to the final image of two women in wide-brimmed hats. Toothy grins stretched the women's cheeks but failed to reach their eyes. Donna recognized the gold loving-cup for the winning garden cradled in one woman's arm.

"Isn't that Margery?" Elizabeth tapped on the image of the woman with the trophy.

On closer inspection, she recognized Margery. Geesh. They did look similar, especially with their garden hats. "Hold my phone for a second."

Donna handed her phone over and darted to the bedroom. A possibility formed in her head as she rushed past Mark, straightening his tie.

"Honey!" he called after her. "Funeral."

She refused to slow down but held up her hand to show she'd heard. If she turned out to be right, he'd find out soon enough. Inside their bedroom, Donna grabbed the crime scene photo envelope, then rushed back past her husband again.

"Got it," she informed Elizabeth and slapped it on the island top. Grabbing the envelope by the bottom, she shook the photos out onto the surface. Her fingers moved over various photos trying to find a specific one, the close-up of Margery and her hat."

"Look at the hat!" Donna's finger stabbed at the hat in the photo.

Elizabeth laid the cell phone down beside the indicated photo. "Looks like the one she wore in the trophy photo."

"Not exactly. Look at the other woman. Notice anything?"

They both leaned over and stared at the photos. Elizabeth spoke first. "You realize I don't know these people. I will say the woman who didn't get the trophy looks a little perturbed despite the smile. It makes me wonder why the other woman looks equally stiff and uncomfortable. After all, she won."

Mark pushed the door open. "You ready, honey?"

"Not yet," she said, her feet carrying her the few steps to her husband's side and pressing his arm affectionately. "Why don't you head out without me? Are you taking Howard?"

"Actually, I am. He thought he might like to see the undercover operation."

It made sense. "I'll see you there. Elizabeth will catch a ride with me. Maybe we could meet up at A Little Bit of Paris." She hesitated as she calculated how long it would take to do the needed sleuthing steps. "At one?"

Mark did a double take. "The funeral won't take that long."

Not wanting to reveal her hunch before she confirmed it, Donna gave his arm a playful pat. "We just enjoyed the delicious, hearty breakfast I made. No one will be hungry before one."

"I guess." He lowered his chin and stared. "You're not doing anything dangerous, are you?"

"Of course not." She forced a laugh. "You know me."

"That's why I asked."

"Such a jokester," she teased. "Have fun at the funeral." She stepped back and gave a finger wave.

Mark held up a hand in farewell, nodded at Elizabeth, and then stepped back into the foyer.

Before speaking, Donna glanced at the door, held a finger to her lips, and said, "Go get ready. I'll explain in the car."

The words sent Elizabeth rushing from the room with the door swinging in her wake. The image on her phone showed the two gardeners with their wide-brimmed hats—rivals forced to stand together for an uncomfortable moment. Despite Elizabeth's comment about all the women looking alike, she recognized the other woman as Miss Emmeline, Margery's neighbor.

Chapter Twenty-Three

THE FRONT DOOR rattled with the violence of the slam. Donna gritted her teeth. Back when she refurbished the inn, she fell in love with the etched glass, oval insert door. It gave the exterior a welcoming feel and allowed sunlight into the foyer. Never did it occur to her that her guests would be slamming out of the place. Nor did she expect a half-dozen murders would occur near or actually in her inn.

Footsteps slapped down the staircase, pulling Donna's attention to witness Elizabeth's descent in a sunflower sundress. Once she reached the foyer, she twirled and asked with bright eyes and the corners of her mouth twitching, "Will this do? It's…" She paused to make air quotes with her fingers. "…the dressiest thing I packed. A funeral wasn't in my plans."

"It will work, especially for a summer funeral. There isn't a dress code. If a person showed up in a pair of cut-off shorts that didn't quite do the job, reeking of body odor and barefoot, they might get a censorious look. Don't expect much attention. Not only will people be watching for a mistress, but they're attending to see if the husband is acting especially bereft. There's also all the folks who don't normally see each other except for funerals and weddings. They'll be catching up and gathering information for gossip."

Her lips pursed and then she whistled. "That's bloody marvelous. It's like one of those daytime serials where the murdered person could have been killed by any of the characters. I'm sure they'll be talking about that."

"For months." Donna shook her head and smirked. "I have no doubt we will nail down the murderer, but all the same, many will still whisper that the husband did it. Wouldn't be surprised if he moves his practice."

Elizabeth, who had been applying lipstick, stopped with her bottom lip coated in the deep rose color. "You don't think the husband is guilty?"

"Not entirely." She smoothed her muted floral dress as she spoke. "Jeff's alibi checks out. Total strangers verified his appearance in New York City at the conference."

"He hired a killer."

"Normally, that would be the easy solution. It would make everyone in town happy since they always prefer an out-of-towner for the crime. None of the locals want to admit they could have been fooled by someone they see on a daily basis."

She inhaled deeply and patted her coif. "I think I bought into Jeff as a player until my mother revealed Margery started those rumors. She wanted people to have a biased opinion of Jeff if she filed for divorce. North Carolina is a no-fault divorce state, and everything gets split fifty-fifty unless there are special circumstances. I'd think a husband as a known philanderer would meet the criteria."

"Wait," Elizabeth popped up her index finger. "Didn't you say he was a big flirt?"

"I did," Donna admitted, but before Elizabeth could launch into why flirting equated infidelity, she continued. "Flirting is part of Southern charm. Well, it was. The young people are more like Northerners, choosing not to engage in the gentle art of flirtation. Most of the time, flattery is used to make people feel better. Those engaged in business use it to sell products."

"Don't people realize they're being lied to?" Elizabeth wrinkled her nose and cocked her head as if trying to untangle a conundrum.

"Maybe. Depends on how subtle the flattery is. All the same, it still makes them feel good."

Elizabeth sniffed. "Not sure why you'd convict anyone for the suspicion of murder due to flirting since all Southerners do it."

"Not all." Donna grimaced. "I don't. Life might be a ton easier if I did. Mark doesn't, but that has more to do with being a cop. As for judging Jeff, it depends on how particular people feel about him. Plenty of serial killers have groupies who believe they're innocent. All the same, I don't think he's guilty, which means someone else committed the murder."

"No hitman?"

Even though the husband was usually guilty, she had her doubts. "There's no reason for him to get rid of his wife. He had a nice house and apparently, his wife allowed him to do whatever he wanted." She cleared her throat and then shouldered her nearby purse and grabbed the seasonal straw hats. "We need to get going. Coming in late will attract attention we don't want. It would be better not to go than arrive late. We can talk in the car."

The two of them hurried through the kitchen, earning a sleepy-eyed glance from Jasper as they moved by. "Be back soon, boy."

It served as her usual response since no matter how long she'd been gone, he reacted the same. Donna hesitated at the back door, debating if she should lock the door. Everyone would be at the funeral, except for the guests who wouldn't welcome being locked out of the inn. All the same, she turned the lock. Those up to no good came through the backdoor. Guests could use the front door with the number lock panel. Surely, they'd be smart enough to carry the key code with them.

In the car, Elizabeth asked, "What changed your mind about the husband's guilt?"

Donna's eyes narrowed as she started the car. "Maybe my mother saying Margery started the rumors. This sounds about right because when a divorce happens, it's viewed as a failure. Margery had a lot of pride in her family line. She refused to take Jeff's name and even insisted that he take the Baumgarten family name. Although, tired of being called Dr. Nutter, he might have made that decision on his own."

"Makes sense. Plenty of Nutters in England. It may have been a common name once, but I suspect many have changed it, not enjoying the comparison to a daft person."

Donna pulled onto the street and pointed the car toward the funeral home. For the most part, the streets weren't busy. Most were at the home, except for the occasional tourist couple or family meandering down the street, clutching shopping bags or ice cream cones, sometimes both. A skeleton crew manned most businesses. Closing wouldn't be an option considering summer was their busy season.

Even though they had a late start, it should be no hardship reaching the funeral home in plenty of time. Donna preferred to see the people milling around the casket during visitation. All the better for interaction and observation than sitting in the back staring at a bunch of heads while a grandchild worked their way through a painful violin solo. The funeral home offered the services of a harpist, who also happened to be the funeral director's wife. She played at most funerals, but to be fair, she could tickle the strings better than most.

"As for Jeff changing his last name, I would if I had that unfortunate surname. The dentist office he shares with another doctor is simply called Legacy Dentistry. Names carry weight in both good and bad ways. As a Tollhouse, I ended up baking."

"Tollhouse? I'd think it would mean someplace you paid a toll."

"Probably did, originally. Now it stands for chocolate chip cookies." Donna stopped at a light as a beautifully restored Packard touring sedan crossed the intersection. It was unusual, but not overly. Classic cars along with car shows reigned supreme among men of a certain age. It often served as a bonding ritual between grandfathers and their teenage grandsons. Behind the Packard came a red Dodge Charger, bearing a 01 on the door and hints of the Rebel flag on the rooftop. It was not a classic in her opinion, but car show fans would gobble it down like Tollhouse cookies.

"Look at the old cars!" Elizabeth announced as she rolled down her window to stick her head outside as if that would allow her a better view. "What's going on?" she asked as a silver DeLorean came into view.

"I suspect a car show. Not here, but maybe the next town over." She watched the cars move through the light slowly. Passers-by stopped on the sidewalk and a few people came out of their businesses for a better look. One, two, three…eight cars went through the light. Normally, if you were lucky, three normal-sized cars could make the light. What was happening?

A motorcycle cop raced beside the cars and waved at one of Legacy's finest, standing near the traffic light pole. Donna, recognizing the cop, waved at him and shouted, "Officer McNeal! What's happening?"

The young officer made his way to Donna's sedan and tipped his hat. "Sorry for the delay, Mrs. Taber. A little boy south of here is battling a deadly disease. All he wanted was to see classic cars ride by his house. He's not well enough to go to the car show. His momma put the suggestion on social media and all these folks showed up. We've been trying to get them all through at once to not break up the parade. Seemed like the right thing to do."

A tear welled up in Donna's eye. She swallowed hard, but she still had a funeral to attend and suspects to eyeball. "Why isn't my side of the light turning green?"

"It will as soon as the last of the classic cars pass. I'll radio it in and then your side will go green."

"Do you know how many cars there might be?" Donna crossed her fingers on the hand not clutching the steering wheel. Maybe the Cadillac Eldorado complete with tail fins was the next-to-last one.

The officer scratched his head. "It's hard to say. I heard a few days ago it might be two hundred. Could be less or more."

Two hundred. Had she heard him, right? Probably. Most classic car owners wouldn't mind a drive to show off their car, especially if it was for a good cause. She rubbed her hand over the wheel as she considered what to do. "We have a funeral to attend." She gestured to Elizabeth. "You do know this is the wife of the visiting Scotland Yard Detective Inspector."

McNeal gave a polite head bob. "How do, ma'am. Hope you're enjoying your stay in our fair city."

Fortunately, Elizabeth pulled in her head to acknowledge the greeting. "I am, thank you."

The young officer beamed and then signaled to the cars behind Donna to back up. "You can turn around and go the other way to the funeral home. It's longer, but not two hundred cars long. Sorry for your trouble."

Donna sighed but thanked the officer before she made a three-point turn. She ended up passing the inn and heading down the coastal road, which seemed to be free of traffic. As they went, she considered how late their detour would make them. A mile down the road, Elizabeth gestured to the realty sign for the luxurious neighborhood they'd visited yesterday.

"We'll be passing Margery's house."

"So?" Donna glanced over at her passenger who'd blinked and then rubbed her hands together. "Obviously, you're thinking something. What is it?"

"Why not check out Margery's garden? Everyone will be at the funeral. Besides, we'll be late anyhow."

It was a good plan. Too bad Donna hadn't thought of it. "How will we get in?"

"We walk over from the other property that's being developed. You mentioned no fences were allowed."

The student learned fast. Elizabeth scored points for her ideas, but she didn't know everything. Donna slowed to make the turn into the neighborhood. "Everyone has those cameras in their yards. How do you get around those?"

Elizabeth smiled as she answered. "We don't. Let's put on our straw hats and sunglasses and casually wander over as if we aren't aware we've crossed any boundary. If anyone questions us, I'll talk using my snootiest upper-crust accent."

It might work. "In the end, they can't arrest us for simply being confused and walking somewhere we shouldn't. For it to be labeled trespassing, intent has to be established. Not sure, but I think there have to be private property signs or at least a fence. If we hurry, we might be able to make it to the home for the parking lot gossip. We have the perfect excuse with the classic car parade. To sell this, we need to park in front of the property we're coming from."

Fortunately, no other cars waited in front of the sparsely wooded lot. Donna parked, exited, and then reached inside the car for the hats. Once properly disguised with hats and glasses, they picked their way through the lot with Elizabeth shouting room suggestions. "I think the atrium should go here!"

Realizing her actions were to establish their purpose, Donna said, "None of the cameras can reach this far, and I'm not sure if they even have sound. Even if they do, the ocean drowns out any conversation." She gestured with her hand. "Still, feel free to meander around."

Getting into her role, Elizabeth turned in circles, shaded her eyes with her hand, looked out toward the sea, and bent to pick a wildflower. Any observers would probably dismiss them as out-of-towners and go about their day. Their modest heels aerated the soil as they picked their way over to Margery's yard. Knowing Jeff still intended to show it for the garden tour, Donna slipped off her heels and Elizabeth did likewise. They padded across the neatly cut grass, listening to the roar of the ocean as they made their way toward the spot where Margery last stood, possibly admiring her garden.

Wisteria perfumed the air with a light sweet note. Colorful lantana blossoms stood out against the green leaves. The flowers registered, but not as much as the figure half-hidden in the shade of a neighboring tree. Donna stiffened, not knowing what to expect. For observational purposes, they accidentally passed an unmarked border. That was their story and hopefully, Elizabeth would stay close while Donna pretended to be an unknown silent stranger.

Chapter Twenty-Four

THE SHADOWY FIGURE under the tree stepped out into the sunlight. Elizabeth gasped, but Donna held her best poker face, remembering her father telling her to never allow an animal to know you're scared of it. The advice worked with people, too, especially the unknown element. The middle-aged woman with short, mussed curls and dirt-smeared capris and shirt had none of the attitude of the warrior queen they'd met the day before who ordered her gardener around and stomped into the Baumgarten home uninvited. Dark circles under her eyes indicated a restless night or maybe more.

Elizabeth must not have made the connection because she dipped her head and then waved her hand to indicate the yard. "Brilliant job on the flower beds."

Instead of a biting comment about them not being her beds and she wasn't the gardener or an accusation about trespassing, Emmeline's soft reply had them both moving closer.

"Margery always had an eye for design." She sniffed and then pushed her shoulders back, showing a streak of the woman they'd met yesterday. "Or maybe someone else had the flair for gardening arrangement. Whomever it was, Margery took that information to the grave with her."

That, she did.

Still, the woman's behavior confused Donna. She'd have sworn at first that the woman might have been crying. Odd. Gossip mentioned stiff competition between tour members that would make an amicable friendship difficult in such close neighbors. Garden tour visitors would comment on the two gardens, possibly in the presence of the owners. Each tour visitor received a scorecard to rate various aspects of the garden, such as color, originality, the inclusion of native plants, flow, and beauty. A box near the end of the garden walkway served as the collection point for the cards. After the two-day tour ended, a club member collected the box contents, which were supposedly used for judging purposes.

Even though Donna had been on the tour previous times, it wasn't until Mark went with her that it was pointed out how the system could easily be manipulated. Since all anyone did was circle numbers to rate the gardens, a participant could stuff the boxes with positive entries, especially since each gardener had to carry their own box inside each night. If nothing else, they could read the entries and know how their garden did and then compare it to the actual results. Someone who had all fives in every category might be suspicious if they came in dead last.

Then again, the cards might be a sop to the general public to let them feel as if they had a say in the matter. It could be judged by a member within the club who could let personal feelings influence them. They might even participate in allowing a different person to win each year, but she rejected that idea as soon as it came. Margery Baumgarten had won several times. Still, on the times Donna had toured, hers had been the best garden. Something about it tended to be more polished with a better flow and yet managed to feel natural.

"Lovely," Elizabeth agreed with a minuscule nod, accompanied by a brittle laugh. "You must forgive us for trespassing."

Donna winced. To admit to it would establish intent. All the same, Elizabeth continued on.

"I just had to see the ocean from here. I live in land-locked London and so seldom see it, especially from this side of the pond."

"It's worth seeing it," Emmeline admitted, turning toward the water with Elizabeth and contemplating the white caps on the waves. It gave Donna the needed opening to move to the area where Margery had been found. With her feet about a foot from the gently gurgling water feature, she glanced toward Emmeline's home. There were plenty of windows, and even a couple of balconies possibly off the bedrooms, including a long, elevated terrace off the second floor. There was easy visibility to notice any happenings in the yard next door, which begged the question, why hadn't Emmeline noticed the body in the yard sooner? Maybe she was outside puttering around in her yard, getting ready for the show. With the similarities of the two women, one could be mistaken for the other if wearing a garden hat.

Both women, obviously done with contemplating, turned back. Elizabeth spoke in a less snooty tone. "We need to be going. Thank you for sharing your view."

Following her lead, Donna padded after her guest as they picked their way over to their original entry spot, donned their shoes, and then continued through the sparsely wooded lot until they reached the car.

Safely hidden away behind the car's sealed windows, Elizabeth exhaled heavily and then giggled. "My first lead on an undercover assignment. Did you get what you needed?"

"Pretty much." She would have liked to stay in the area a bit longer and try out various angles, including Emmeline's yard, but that would be pushing it too much. "I'm surprised she didn't threaten to call the police for trespassing."

"Not sure she could, considering she, too, was in the yard. Makes you wonder if she made a habit of wandering in the yard next door or only picked it up recently. Perhaps morbid curiosity brought her over."

"You're right." How could she have missed such a detail? Disgusted with herself, Donna started the car. "Plenty of people turn into looky-loos when faced with a scene of a crime."

Her phone rang as they made their slow exit from the neighborhood of opulent homes and convoluted relationships. Simon's name showed on the small dash console that displayed phone numbers. Excited to hear what her stepfather had discovered on his golfing venture, she pushed the accept button. "Donna here. Go ahead."

"I just have a moment," Simon's smooth and collected voice came through the speakers. "I told my golf buddies I needed to check in with the old ball and chain. Don't repeat that to your mother, please. Just guy talk."

"No worries." She understood sometimes you had to talk the talk to get the information you wanted. No one would doubt that Simon adored her mother. "What do you have for me?"

"Okay. Gordon confirmed he signed two multi-million-dollar whole life policies for both a husband and wife about six months ago. Joked about them paying through the nose since they weren't twenty-something anymore."

"Who?"

"Locals."

"Could you pinpoint it a little more?"

Simon huffed. "You do know this stuff is supposed to be secret. A person needs to be able to trust their agent. You're better off going with who could afford such a policy. Gordon did say the premiums ran about 200,000 dollars per year for each. That would be 400,000 together. Who has that type of pocket change?"

Probably the people in the neighborhood they had just left.

However, a few of them were probably fending off creditors since things weren't always how they looked. Still, Simon had gone to bat for her. "Good job. I appreciate it. I'll have to make you something yummy."

"Strawberry Chiffon Pie would suit."

Of course it would. It was one of her most labor-intensive concoctions, but to be fair, Simon wouldn't know that. "Will do. Talk to you later."

She hung up the phone and drove for about five seconds before she grumbled, "Doggone it!"

"Dog, what?" Elizabeth queried while peering out the windows. "I don't see a dog anywhere."

"It's an expression." Donna frowned as she tightened her grip on the steering wheel. "I pride myself on reading people, and I would have sworn Jeff wasn't guilty—no matter how he looked after the death of his wife. Now, with two huge life insurance policies…"

"That was six months ago."

"All the better to throw the police off the trail. An accidental death would have been better, but that didn't work out. A person who just buys a policy on his wife before killing her shouts guilty. The insurance company usually helps by giving up pertinent information since they don't want to pay a killer. A policy for both of them sounds normal and certainly would have the intended victim signing without being too suspicious." She shook her head slowly. "Can't believe I called that wrong."

"Wait." Elizabeth leaned over the console to nudge Donna. "What I have seen so far is you're an excellent sleuth with access to many avenues of gathering information. I envy you. Don't cave to the easy the-husband-did-it. Was there a prenup? If so, it's binding after death. Just because a not-so-young couple bought big life policies, it doesn't mean it was Margery and Jeff."

"You're right." Donna felt buoyed by Elizabeth's confidence in her. She tapped the gas pedal as the car turned onto the coastal road. "We can still make it to the funeral home. The problem is, I've been thinking inside the box. What if Margery wasn't the intended victim?"

Chapter Twenty-Five

P ARKED CARS LITTERED both sides of the road as Donna and Elizabeth approached the Eternal Rest Funeral Home. It was odd that so many folks were in one spot. It could be a family reunion. Despite craning her neck to survey the area, no colorful bounce houses or blow-up water slides dotted any of the residential yards. There were no signs of activity at the middle school that squatted directly across from the funeral home. Donna slowed as she approached the entrance of the Eternal Rest Funeral Home and turned into the parking lot, only to find it filled.

"Seriously?" she grumbled to herself as she made another slow turn of the parking lot.

Elizabeth pivoted in her seat in an effort to help find an elusive, empty parking spot. "It looks like Margery was well-loved."

While the Baumgarten family had lived in Legacy as long as there had been a town, Margery never struck her as a philanthropist, but she made enough public contributions not to be called Scrooge. As for volunteer work, there was nothing unusual. She showed up once a month as a Friends of the Library volunteer who sorted donated books. No children. No living parents. Just a handful of shirt-tail relatives made up her family. That information came via Mark.

"Nope. Nothing like the promise of being witness to a major scene to bring people out."

"Look! There's Howie." Elizabeth waved wildly at two familiar figures standing outside the main door. Both men stood near the entrance of the home, talking. Mark waved her down.

Donna slowed the car and stopped beside the men, and then rolled down her window. "Hey, y'all."

Her husband tapped his watch. "I was starting to get worried."

"Classic car parade," she offered as an explanation, not willing to go into details. "There's no place to park? Is the funeral over?"

"Lucky for you, due to the huge turnout, it hasn't even started. Everyone wants to get a gander at Margery, another look at the grieving husband, and to notice any woman who might be comforting him a little bit too much."

While Mark's summary did ring true, it made the locals sound a bit peculiar. Donna shot a pained smile in Elizabeth's direction and said, "Not a whole lot to do around here, which explains a funeral being the *it* activity."

"Wait," Mark held up one finger, opened the entrance door, stuck his head inside and said something indecipherable, resulting in one of the younger officers popping out. "Officer Kaminski will park your car and allow you to get inside before the funeral starts."

Feeling a bit bad about the young officer having to search for a parking place, Donna thanked him, put the car in park, and exited with Elizabeth. The two went inside followed by their husbands.

Mark wrapped his arm around his wife, allowing his lips to be close to her ear. "Nothing of note so far with the exception of an overwhelming number of visitors. They descended on the respite dining room like a plague of locusts, devouring everything in sight."

The mention of food jerked her to a stop. "Oh no! I forgot to bring any edibles."

"Just as well. I doubt any of the food went to actual relatives or valued friends. Besides, you already gave away my praline cheese-cake."

"I don't remember seeing your name on it," she teased. "I'll make another."

By that time, a medium hum of voices spilled out of the large parlor. Small groups and couples loitered in the hall near huge fish tanks featuring angelfish swimming elegantly through their well-appointed environment as if they didn't have a care in the world. The soft spill of water from the tank filters created a soothing white noise that muffled most conversations.

A quick visual survey revealed nothing of note, except some impatience by individuals indicated by pointed glances at the wall-mounted clock, staring out windows, pacing, and even some heated discussions about staying versus leaving. Donna caught up on one argument and secretly bet on the wife, who insisted they should stay. Caught up in the couple's debate, she almost missed the man staggering out of the parlor, using the wall to stay standing. He collapsed on a nearby loveseat and wrapped his arms around his stomach. As a former nurse, she recognized medical distress, although she wasn't clear on the identity of the man.

"Mark, I'm going to see what's going on with him."

Her footsteps made no sound on the thick carpet as she hurried to the man's side. She knelt beside the chair. "Are you okay? I'm a nurse."

The man gasped heavily and looked up at Donna. "I have no clue. Horrible stomach cramps." He wiggled his fingers. "My fingers tingle as do my toes." He shook his head slowly. "The past week I've been so sick. I made an effort to come since my uncaring wife refused to do so. Felt someone should since Margery was our neighbor. She was always a good neighbor."

The pain in his eyes testified to his grief. His flushed skin could be the result of combined shock and loss, but something else could be the problem, too. Donna spoke before taking hold of the man's wrist, "I'm going to take your pulse."

His pulse hovered in the normal range, but sweat beaded on his forehead and lip. "You need to go to the hospital."

"Oh no!" He forced out his protestation through clenched teeth. 'I just need to cool off." He waved his hand in front of his face. "Too many people. It's too hot inside."

Donna's medical knowledge along with the man's symptoms had her gesturing for her husband. Obviously waiting for such an action, he dashed over, darting through a half-dozen bored children who engaged in a game of catchers around the fish tank.

"What is it?" Mark asked in his uncanny, constant calm voice.

"This man needs to go to the hospital ASAP. Can one of the officers drive him? I don't want to wait for an ambulance."

"Can do."

Mark pulled out his phone and started scrolling through it, while the man in question sputtered. "No hospital. No police car."

Donna would have sworn it was impossible for his face to grow any whiter, but it did. At the same time, conversations around them stopped. No doubt they'd be the second act. She leaned forward and kept her voice low. "You've been poisoned. We need to get you medical care immediately, or you'll die."

He sighed, "I can't die. If I do, she wins."

"Who?" both Mark and Donna asked in unison.

"The woman who poisoned me—Emmeline, my wife."

Chapter Twenty-Six

A BIRD TWEETED in one of the several trees the funeral home-owner had planted around his building in an effort to soften the lines and give it a peaceful feel. Snippets of conversation drifted across the parking lot as Donna and Mark supported the stumbling man, who identified himself as Roger Dalton. Between them, they drunk walked him to the waiting squad car where Kaminski, one of Legacy's newest officers, stood beside the open back door.

Roger clutched the open car door frame, resisting getting into the back of the police car. Most people would. After all, riding in the back indicated bad life choices.

Donna, who had served as his left side support, attempted to reassure him. "I'll ride in the back with you."

The tension that kept his spine ramrod straight melted away, and he bent and crawled into the vehicle without a word. Fortunately, the sedan had a roomy back seat, allowing Donna to join Roger but with reasonable space in between. It would be tricky, but, if need be, she could start emergency life-saving measures.

Mark stuck his head into the open car door to give instructions. "Kaminski, hold the siren until you get a quarter-mile away."

"Will do, sir." The officer gave a strong reply and a nod.

Once Mark slammed the door, the car shifted into motion, making its way around the gawkers who came out to observe the action. Not using the siren so near the funeral home was a courtesy for the mourners. The event would be talked about for years to come. There was no need to add to the chaos. Besides, lights only usually got motorists to move to the side while checking their speedometer for assurance they weren't the problem. As loud as sirens could be, an occasional motorist never budged an inch. Loud music or headphones impaired their ability to hear them. It didn't help that some current music actually had sirens in it. If the unaware motorist ever noticed, it wasn't until the police vehicle swerved around them. There were the same issues with ambulances, and Donna had heard plenty from the EMTs when she worked at the hospital.

Even though Donna no longer clocked in to work the post-surgery floor at the hospital, she knew the information the emergency room would want. "Roger." She spoke his name to get his attention, but it had no effect. His body sank back into the upholstery, and if it wasn't for the shoulder restraint, he might have tipped over.

"Roger!" she repeated, shaking the man, whose open eyes stared at the back of the headrest in front of him.

"What!" He barked the reply and shook off her hand.

Normally, Donna would regard such behavior as rude, but since he believed his spouse was trying to kill him, she'd overlook his sharp retort.

"Do you know what toxin you ingested?" Donna knew he probably didn't, but it was a required question. "Maybe you were using a chemical compound to rid your place of rats or other pests?"

"Rats? Emmeline would have a heart attack if we had rats in our home." He chuckled and then it dissolved into a choking, gasping fit that had Donna pounding his back.

Goodness, he might be worse off than she anticipated. Leaning forward over the front seat, she addressed Kaminski. "You need to call it in. Poisoning. We needed medical personnel ready."

The officer tapped on the dash screen and spoke. "This is car 812 headed to the hospital with a male senior citizen suffering from poisoning."

Roger, who Donna feared might be unresponsive, jerked and then snapped, "I'm not a senior citizen! I'm in the prime of my life and career."

Good, the remark about being a senior energized him. There was no need to point out if he was fifty and over, he earned the dubious title of senior. "Roger, tell me about your career."

The man turned a perplexed face toward Donna as if trying to figure out her words. It could be the poison was slowing the thought processes and even recognition of everyday words. She wanted to get back to whatever he'd ingested or injected, but she'd be willing to come around the other way to get the information. While most people enjoyed talking about themselves, that didn't stretch to discussing someone trying to kill them. "What do you do for a living?"

"Architect. I designed the Ashville Library."

"Impressive." She cooed the word, attempting to sound awed despite the fact she had never seen it. All she had to do was keep him talking. "Sounds like a great job. Did you always want to be an architect?"

"No." He shook his head slowly. "Gardening was my thing, but you know, gardeners don't make any money." He sighed and stared at the window.

Poor man. Donna patted his hand that rested on his knee. Normally, she wouldn't be so forward, but faced with possible death, the man must be reviewing his life choices and wondering if he'd made the right ones. If he had a reason to live, he'd fight harder to live. So far, it didn't sound like his wife would serve that purpose. "You could still garden, especially in that lovely, big yard of yours."

Her comment only earned a snort, and so far, she had no useful information. It was time to cut to the chase. "How did your wife poison you?"

"If I knew that, I wouldn't be in a police car heading to the hospital."

He had a point but not a helpful one. Her hand slipped from his knee in case he got the wrong idea. "Think. Anything different or unusual in what you ate or drank? It could be something you touched, too. Some toxins react immediately on contact. Did you feel a burning sensation on your fingers?"

While many toxins were absorbed through the skin, such as mercury and nicotine, the results took a while to show. A caustic acid might burn, but a person would react to it. Most would race to the shower or even to the emergency room. Apparently, Roger wasn't too worried, or he wouldn't be attending a neighbor's funeral. Maybe he was a typical guy who waited to the very last minute to seek assistance.

Trying not to be too obvious, Donna used her peripheral vision to monitor her involuntary charge while pulling her phone out of her purse. A glowing icon alerted her to a message from Elizabeth, wondering where she'd vanished to. Leaving Elizabeth at a funeral of a woman she'd never met ranked right up there as a less than gracious entertainer. From her left came a grumbling sound.

Roger's eyes rolled upward, and his hands fisted. He stiffened and then turned to Donna to speak. At the same time, the siren sounded and Kaminski sped up, darting around drivers who refused to pull over for the flashing lights and sirens. In the back seat, both Roger and Donna swayed side to side with the motion. The screech of the siren filled the car, wiping out the possibility of hearing any whispered words.

Roger's lips moved, but Donna couldn't hear anything. She shouted, "What?"

Her concentration remained on his lips as he enunciated a word. Mercy, why had she never taken lip-reading or was it sign language? If it were sign language, then Roger would have to know it, too. As she swayed in place, she tried imitating the motion of his lips. "Brrrr," she managed the first part of the word.

Bread. He had eaten bread. That was the culprit. It often destroyed most dieter's attempts to cut calories. She shouted "Bread!"

Kaminski slowed to ask, "What did you say?"

"Keep going. I'm not talking to you."

As a cook, she should know all sorts of edibles that started with *brr.* "Bratwurst?" She directed the loud comment to Roger but knew as soon as she said it that it would be difficult for a poisoner to put the toxin into the sausage without actually making the sausage. Most killers chose something liquid because it would be easy to mix the toxin in—something with a strong flavor that would cover the tang of the toxin. Plenty of spy shows featured a buxom female spy flipping open her poison ring and emptying the toxin inside into a martini or a glass of wine to serve to the handsome counterspy. It worked well in the movies and would in real life, especially if the target imbibed on a regular basis.

The word *bratwurst* caused Roger to grimace and shake his head. On the upside, he could hear her. What would a successful architect in the prime of life be drinking?

"Brandy?"

His eyes lit up in recognition, and then his chin plopped down to his chest as the car jerked into the emergency lane of the hospital.

Blue scrub-attired employees waited by the emergency door with a wheelchair. They'd need a gurney now.

DONNA PACED THE post-surgery waiting room. There were thirteen steps one way and fifteen the other, which meant it wasn't a perfect square. How sad that Roger had no one waiting to see if he'd be okay. Mark managed to get a search order from the judge who was at the funeral and welcomed a reason to leave since it was already an hour late starting. By that time, Roger's wife would know something was up because the police would be tossing the house. Even though Donna had emphasized *brandy*, there could be other things Roger hadn't even considered. Spouses accepted vitamin capsules from their significant others and suspected nothing. Never mind that this was the first time their spouse had done such a thing. Thinking the worst of everyone was a horrible way to live.

A nurse in cartoon printed scrubs wearing a surgery-style cap and mask entered the room and waved at her. Familiar eyes, but Donna had trouble placing her with so little of her showing.

The nurse in question moved closer and hissed, "It's me, Elizabeth."

Donna did a double take. "So, it is." Using her hand, she gestured to the scrubs, hat, and mask. "What's with the disguise?"

"I needed to get into the hospital." She pulled down her mask to talk more easily. "Howard tagged along with Mark. They left me at the inn and out of the action. Fortunately, Thelma was there and helped me round up the disguise. She used to work at a children's rehab facility or something. It was easy sneaking in and finding you. No one bothered to stop me."

"Great job," Donna offered while pondering where Thelma had

worked before. There was no need to mention to Elizabeth that no one had stopped her because there was no need to do so. Even when visitors stayed past visiting hours, security never bothered to escort them out.

"How come you got to stay?" Elizabeth asked, curious about Donna's total lack of costume.

"I brought him." She didn't tack on she was a nurse or that Legacy Memorial Hospital had few security breaches, spies, or even murderers slipping up the stairs, which made for a more relaxed atmosphere.

"That's a good reason. Do they think you're a relative?"

One insurance agent had tried to get Donna to complete the necessary paperwork. Thankfully, Roger had an insurance card in his wallet along with his driver's license which answered most of the required questions. She dithered when they got to who to call in an emergency, which this most definitely was. Did he have children? If he did, they'd want to know about dear old dad.

An unsmiling, unfamiliar nurse swung open the door to the waiting room and glared at Elizabeth. "You need to go back to your floor. I'm tired of nurses from other departments sneaking over here to goof off."

"She's on break," Donna offered when Elizabeth's eyes grew as large as a puppy caught in the middle of destroying treasured property. "By the way, is Roger Dalton in a room yet?"

Formidable Nurse sniffed and asked, "Who are you?"

Thank goodness this was someone she'd never met—possibly someone who thought living in a coastal city would be Heaven on earth. Any other staff person would recognize her. Might as well take advantage of her ignorance. Her chin went up as she delivered a cool gaze. "I'm his cousin. I brought him in. I'd like to see him."

A long silence stretched between them until the nurse spoke. "He's asleep. Probably just as well for him. The doctor wants him to stay overnight. I'm sure the doctor will come by to talk to you, or is there someone else more closely related?" She peered around the empty room as if someone might pop up behind the rose-colored leatherette loveseat or from behind the potted plant.

"I'm it for now. I'd still like to see him, if only to reassure myself he's resting easy."

Since Donna used to be head nurse at one time, she knew they didn't tolerate fools or the weak-kneed. Most might have been discouraged, but Donna saw it as a challenge and crossed her arms. That's right, read that body language.

"Room 218 on the west wing." She turned with a military pivot, saying a great deal about where she may have served last.

The glass door allowed them to watch the nurse move back to her station before they moved themselves. "Follow me," Donna instructed. She held a finger up to her mouth before turning left. There was no need to count the rooms since she knew her way around. They were almost to the room when another scrub-dressed nurse spotted Elizabeth and motioned to her.

"Come here. I need some help."

"Not my floor." Elizabeth recycled her previous excuse and shot Donna a beseeching look.

"It won't take long. With your accent, I bet my patient will think she died and woke up in London." The woman winked. "I'll buy you a cup of coffee later for being a good sport."

Elizabeth padded reluctantly after the coffee-buying nurse, glancing back every other step at Donna. One of the perils of going undercover is having to do routine tasks that your disguise announced you'd be proficient at. When someone grabs a new nurse or a temp, it was to do a job no one else wanted to do. Donna only hoped no needles would be involved. If there were, she was certain Elizabeth would confess her ploy or possibly faint. Dropping into a dead faint worked in most situations if a person could steel themselves before hitting the hard floor.

A woman exited the elevator garbed in a man's trench coat, ball cap, and sunglasses. The outfit screamed *wrong*. Sure, no thinking woman would wear a ball cap with a trench coat. Never mind that the thermometer was at ninety with full humidity. Add in the sunglasses and it equaled a person who didn't want to be recognized.

Unlike Donna, this person didn't know her way around and stopped to stare at each name holder beside the door. If she'd take the sunglasses off, she might see better. Donna flattened her body inside an alcove that often stored cleaning equipment and peeked out to track the suspicious woman. As Donna expected, she turned into 218.

It was time to call the cavalry. Donna pulled out her phone and speed dialed her husband. He picked up on the first ring. "Is he awake?"

"No, but he's got company, and it isn't the friendly sort. Room 218. I thought you needed to know."

Before her husband could warn her not to do anything, she disconnected the phone, knowing good and well if she had the opportunity to stop something bad from happening, she would do it. After all, common decency demanded it, but at the same time, she had to be sure not to get hurt, or she'd never hear the end of it.

Not knowing if the oddly dressed visitor merely wanted to ascertain Roger's condition or had more deadly motives, Donna speed walked to the room and opened the closed door softly. Just in time she witnessed the visitor picking up a pillow and position it over the sleeping Roger's head, saying, "I can't take a chance of you confessing all before you die. So, I'll just hurry it along."

"Oh no you won't!" Donna flew across the room, grabbing the pillow the woman kept a firm grip on. The two of them tussled as if having a pillow fight with one pillow. They shoved one another, bumping into the bed and hitting almost every piece of furniture in the room. Normally, beeps, buzzes, and television game shows poured from patients' rooms along with the squeak of carts. Donna heard nothing but heavy panting, which she suspected was hers.

Adrenalin-fueled, Donna managed to back the would-be smotherer up to the coat rack and snagged the hat, revealing long, black hair. It was not Emmeline. The surprise that it wasn't Emmeline stopped Donna for a brief second, but the lapse was enough for her opponent to press her advantage. Boxing both ears, she stunned Donna and then fled toward the door where Formidable Nurse stood beside a security guard.

Donna pointed at the woman. "Stop her! She just tried to smother Roger."

The woman spun and pointed to an awake Roger. "I curse the day I met you!"

"Same here," a red-faced Roger growled. "Not surprised you're inept at knocking me off. Just my luck I hired a hitwoman who couldn't hit the side of the barn. Instead of doing your job, you killed the woman I *did* love."

"Is that your excuse for not paying me?" the woman screamed back, jerking off her sunglasses. The sound of running feet in the hallway meant the cavalry had arrived. "You can't just contract for me to kill your wife and then not pay me."

"I don't pay for shoddy work."

The remark sent the woman flying toward Roger. Before Donna

could peel herself off the wall that held her up, uniformed officers swarmed the room, grabbing the bad shot hitwoman.

Before they could leave, Donna called out. "Excuse me! Roger Dalton confessed to hiring that woman to kill his wife. Apparently, she's a bad shot and took out Margery Baumgarten instead." She gestured to the nurse and guard. "They heard it, too."

"Okay." The officer acknowledged her statement. "I'll leave an officer here on guard and I believe your husband will be taking a statement."

"Thanks." She waved goodbye as the hitwoman shouted back, "I'm not a bad shot! All middle-aged women look alike."

Formidable Nurse placed a hand on her arm and Donna winced. "Are you okay?"

"Sure, I'm fine, outside of the fact that my husband might be a teeny bit upset with me. Maybe you might not tell him about my pillow fight with a killer. Then there's the fact that I have to explain to my British visitor that my town isn't a regular daytime serial. By the way, where is Elizabeth?"

Epilogue

THE SUN SHONE full force in the late afternoon, melting ice cream cones and crisping first-time beachgoers. As a Southerner, Donna knew the value of air conditioning and knowing when to retreat inside. It was not so with her British guests, who were determined to soak up as much sunshine as possible, which meant the celebratory dinner would be held outside. Elizabeth requested a typical Southerner dinner, which threw Donna for a loop. There were foods attributed to Southerners that most didn't eat, such as pickled pigs' feet. Footsteps warranted a backward look.

Donna witnessed Thelma drifting by with a pleased expression. Normally, her assistant's demeanor hovered somewhere between thoughtful and perplexed when she wasn't predicting dire consequences. "What's got you looking like the cat who lapped up the cream?"

"Closure," she murmured as she stepped nearer. "I just came from a psychic reading with Jeff, Margery's husband."

"Jeff does readings, now?" Donna teased, pretty much knowing what Thelma meant.

"No." She pursed her lips as if trying to judge the sincerity of the inquiry. "I did. He said he needed closure."

"Séance?" Donna wondered aloud since closure with the dead might prove problematic with them being gone and all. "Perhaps he wanted to assure himself Margery didn't blame him for anything."

"Maybe. Not sure. Usually the reader," Thelma paused to point to herself, "doesn't always ask what the seeker needs to hear. It's often too personal. Besides, the spirits know."

"Okay," Donna glanced out at her dinner table that was not quite ready, while struggling with her rampant curiosity. "What did Margery say?"

"It's not for you to know." Thelma shook an index finger at her employer. "If Jeff wanted you to know he would have invited you to the reading. Safe to say, I did my part. How good of terms they parted on will be revealed by the will."

With that pronouncement, Thelma waved and then went on her way, leaving, for a change, a sputtering Donna in her wake.

"Talk about talking and saying nothing." She blew out an audible breath and returned to ready the dinner table for their Southern meal. A plate of freshly sliced tomatoes joined the sweating, tall pitcher of sweet tea waiting on the sunflower-strewn tablecloth. She was not sure what the insect situation was in London, but flies waited, hovering in the shade of the majestic oak tree that arched over the small patio. A small screen cover went over the tomatoes. Mark exited the dining room, carrying a huge platter of golden fried chicken. Even the Colonel's secret herbs and spices had nothing on her own recipe. As the two of them ferried items from the dining room staging area to the patio, they garnered envious glances from a couple playing Scrabble in the dining room as opposed to the game parlor. At last check, the other guests were watching cars run endless laps around a track while creating the maximum amount of noise while doing so, which explained the Scrabble players' defection to another room.

The last items to reach the table were the hot biscuits and milk gravy. Before she could even summon her guests, they drifted through the open French doors and onto the patio.

Howard patted his stomach. "I'm famished. I haven't eaten for days."

That was not exactly the truth. Donna witnessed the man put away enough breakfast to shame a lumberjack. All the same, both he and Mark had probably skipped lunch with the funeral and figuring out Margery's homicide and the premeditated attempted murder of Roger.

"You're in luck," Donna replied. "We've got plenty to eat. Of course, both Elizabeth and I will expect information in return for food."

"Really?" His face puckered up as if he had bitten into an unripe persimmon, and he turned to Mark. "Is this a thing?"

"Absolutely." He winked at Donna and explained, "I have to say it was probably part of our courtship. Donna bribed me with excellent coffee and some mouth-watering creation she'd made that day while we talked about whatever case I was working on."

"What about confidentiality?" Howard inquired as he pulled out a seat for his wife and then slid into the chair next to her.

"I trust my wife," Mark said as he picked up the tea pitcher and filled the glasses. "Donna understands what information shouldn't get out and does a great job of safeguarding it from the gossips in our town. She also uses the gossips to obtain the information I can't."

The words made Donna beam at her husband. Sure, he trusted her not to share the details of his work, but he had never publicly announced it before and in front of Howard, who wasn't entirely cool with it. *Take that*, she thought as she gave the green beans a good stir to make sure the crumbled bacon mixed throughout. Often toppings went to the first person to dig into a serving dish.

The tea poured, Mark helped Donna remove the screen covers and then sat and passed the food. For a few minutes, only the sound of spoons scraping bowls or the occasional murmured thank you sounded as the next dish showed up. Not too surprisingly, the scratch of dog nails on the patio pavers indicated a very enterprising Jasper had figured out where they were and managed to get a guest to open the door.

"Look who's here," Donna pointed out in an amused tone as Jasper sat beside the guests and canted his head upward, using his most pitiful expression. "Don't feed him or you'll have no peace the entire meal. Contrary to his behavior, he's already eaten. Gobbled down some pulled chicken and half a biscuit in the kitchen in conjunction with his dog food. Just don't make eye contact, and he'll get bored."

Following her advice, Howard and Elizabeth applied themselves to their meals with gusto, which pleased Donna, but made it hard to solicit information. The gravy gushed over her potatoes, touching the biscuit, which she prodded out of the way with her finger. At least her husband would spill the details.

"What did you find at Roger and Emmeline's house?"

"Enough arsenic to kill an army of rats. Apparently ordered from the Internet. She admitted she delayed reporting Margery's death because those who report deaths are usually blamed."

A derisive snort escaped Donna's lips. "That's only true if the person has motivation. More likely she didn't want a scrutiny of her own felonious activities. With Jeff being gone, she probably decided it would look odd if she didn't report it. Why didn't Roger call? Anything else?"

Mark arched his shaggy brows as he sipped his lemonade, then returned the glass to the table. "Roger made a point of being out of town when his hired assassin did her job to solidify his alibi. Told several folks he'd be in Ashville working on a project. It would have been better for Margery if he had stayed to point out the target. Anyhow, we took the brandy and gathered up supplements Roger had because they were in capsule form. The entire time Emmeline dogged our steps, explaining Roger had it coming."

With a half-eaten chicken leg in hand, Howard interjected, "That part I couldn't believe. She didn't even try to hide her involvement. Americans are bold, especially the murderers."

Donna felt compelled to point out, "Technically, Roger isn't dead. I'm sure he'll have organ damage. Did the doctors say anything to you about what they found?"

Mark harrumphed and helped himself to more potatoes as he spoke. "There was a hundred times the amount of arsenic in Roger than what would be found normally. He was definitely poisoned. Possibly for a while, too. An official lab report will nail down how long Roger had been ingesting arsenic. From what I gathered from Roger, he took Margery's death hard. That's when he started drinking the tainted brandy. At one point, he must have been suspicious because he commented that Emmeline didn't complain about his drinking—for once." He shook his head and grimaced. "Remind me never to get you mad at me. I happen to know you'd be much more discreet with your methods."

Saying such a thing might strike most people as morbid. Due to the many murder cases they'd shared, Donna did know various ways to murder someone. Along with the motivations, she also understood why they hadn't succeeded. Such knowledge could make her deadly, her husband often teased.

"You're right, I would be." She smirked in his direction. "Fortunately, you've never gotten on my bad side."

Both Mark and Donna chuckled while Elizabeth managed a nervous titter that announced uncertainty about laughing over such a thing.

No real information was offered, except that Emmeline had followed the police through her house, which meant Donna needed to poke some more. "I don't understand Emmeline's motivation. She acted rather despondent when she caught us trespassing in Margery's garden."

At the revelation, Mark merely raised his shaggy brows while Howard yelled, "You did what?"

So much for the old British reserve. There was no reason for her newest friend to take the brunt of the blame. "It's my fault."

"No," Elizabeth sniffed. "Don't take my one moment of inspiration from me. I suggested it."

After confessing, she sat up a little straighter while her husband murmured something indecipherable under his breath. He might be rethinking allowing his wife to make the trip in the first place.

While Donna and Mark had no clue what he said, his wife definitely did, and a wide smile crossed her face. "No, I wasn't being foolish. We discovered Emmeline lurking around the area where Margery was shot. She could have been looking for shell casings."

"She wasn't the murderer," Howard clarified with a superior air.

Before he could say anything else that might have Donna not offering him a piece of the rhubarb apple pie, Donna turned to her husband. "Did she give any reason why she was trying to kill her husband? They've been married a quarter of a century, and she had plenty of time to do it before now."

"True enough." Mark cleared his throat and added, "She never had a reason until she discovered her husband had been helping Margery with her various garden designs. The two were conspiring against Emmeline. As you know, Margery took her share of wins. Then, to find out her own husband was undermining her efforts pushed Emmeline over the edge."

"That's bloody awful. Murder over gardening," Howard declared and then snorted, perhaps being thankful he didn't have to deal with such people on a daily basis.

"Not quite," Elizabeth tapped her tea glass with a spoon to get attention before her husband launched into a rant, which he showed signs of warming up to. "Often, what looks like people going crazy over a simple thing is actually a series of events. Obviously, Emmeline and Roger didn't get along all that well. Maybe gardening honors matter to her a little too much. That much is true. All the same, to find out her own husband was undermining her efforts with someone he was having an affair with had to sting."

Mark picked up his tea glass and held it up to salute Elizabeth. "Good summary. I say you have the makings of a good sleuth."

The sound of a fork hitting the plate drew all eyes to a white-faced Howard. Perhaps the thought of having a wife as independent and opinionated as Donna scared him. Then again, it might be exactly what he needed to realize. The possibility pleased Donna, but she did her best not to show it. Instead, she speculated, asking, "What about Roger?"

"He did plenty of finger pointing," Mark said, reaching for a biscuit. He continued to speak as he buttered it. "He told me he knew his days were numbered once he signed the multi-million-dollar life insurance policy."

The stupid things people do perplexed Donna. Still, she asked, "Why did he sign it? He could have refused."

"I'd think anyone with common sense would, but he probably thought he could outsmart his wife and have the last laugh."

"Sounds about right," Donna agreed. "Even with a questionable hitwoman, people were bound to wonder about a murder. After all, this isn't the big city where you have a shooting every weekend."

"That's the truth. He'll be charged with premeditated murder, even though it ended up being the wrong victim." He reached for the tomatoes and forked a few beefy slices onto his plate. "There's a guard on his room, but I doubt he'll be going anywhere with the exception of prison."

"Just as well," Howard added. "People who kill for silly excuses don't deserve to walk among the rest of us."

Even though he didn't say it, Donna somehow heard *Americans* as opposed to *people*, which ruffled her feathers a wee bit. Okay, make that a lot. "No one in Britain is murdered for stupid reasons?"

Even though she addressed the question to Howard, Elizabeth answered. "All the time. I like to think there's never a good reason for murder. There's someone who got their feelings hurt decades ago and never quite got over it, or someone else finds a rare flower before the murderer did. Then you have the elderly choir member who shot the baritone behind her during practice."

"Oh my!" Donna gasped and pressed a hand over her heart. "Lover's quarrel?"

"Oh, no. He sang off-key. All the time. For the last thirty years. Somehow, she felt it was justified. A few in the choir took her side." All four of them chuckled.

When the laughter died down, Mark said, "You know, we have some free time before you head back to London. Maybe we could head up to Ashville and get in some fly-fishing. Ladies, how about it?"

Her husband knew how she felt about fishing. She preferred her fish not wiggling, already gutted, and sealed in cellophane. What she needed was a diplomatic way to get out of it.

"Oh, Donna!" Elizabeth wiggled her fingers. "We have that *thing*."

It was strange how she said the *thing* like it should mean something. It could be fighting over a pillow with a hired killer—albeit, a mediocre one, but still a killer—could sap a person's memory. She repeated the word. "Thing?"

"You know," Elizabeth hissed. "The super-secret Southern Women Only Tradition."

She had forgotten all about that in her effort to track down Margery's killer. Surely her mother would come up with a satisfactory plan. Donna placed a finger to her lips and nodded.

Mark nudged her under the table, which meant he would ask later.

SOFT FLUTE MUSIC interspersed with bird calls and the sound of running water created a relaxing environment. Employees in crisp slate-gray uniforms with white piping padded around the women in luxurious white robes, resting on thermal loungers. Cucumber slices covered their eyelids. On one side of the spa, a waterfall flowed into a waiting pool where one of the guests waded.

Donna's tension melted away. Running a B and B, cooking up scrumptious meals, and the occasional fight with a killer made life interesting, but sometimes a gal just needed to indulge herself.

She put up her hand to get one of the attendants' attention and turned in Elizabeth's direction to ask, "More mint water? Or do you prefer coconut?"

"Mint, please."

The attentive attendant delivered the flavored water without being asked, pulling an appreciative sigh from Elizabeth. "This place is brilliant. I loved the sea salt scrub and the hot stone massage. Do Southern women do this often?"

Donna's mother, who relaxed on her other side, answered in a mellow tone. "Not nearly enough."

"Sounds lovely," Elizabeth concurred. "If I come back to visit, could we do this again?"

She was already planning her return trip and Donna liked the sounds of it. Elizabeth, she could tolerate. Howard, on the other hand, had yet to grow on her. Perhaps Mark found something endearing about the man. "I'm sure we could arrange it."

"How about another murder?" Elizabeth teased.

Never did she plan for murder, it just happened. "You can never tell."

THE END

Two Many Sleuths Recipes

Southern Lemonade Cocktail Recipe

What Elizabeth drank at the Croaking Frog and became giggly.

PREP TIME: 5 minutes
TOTAL TIME: 5 minutes
YIELD: 6 8 OZ SERVINGS

Ingredients
- Ice
- 16 oz Lemonade
- 6 oz Bourbon
- 4 oz Citron Vodka
- 4 oz Limoncello Liquor
- 16 oz Ginger Ale
- Lemon slices for garnish
- Lime slices for garnish
- Mint sprigs for garnish

Directions
1. Fill a pitcher halfway with ice and lemon and lime slices (one to two lemons and limes, to taste).
2. Add 16 ounces of prepared lemonade, 6 ounces of bourbon, 4 ounces of Citron vodka, and 4 ounces of limoncello; stir.
3. Top with 16 ounces of ginger ale.
4. To serve:
5. Add a cube or two of ice to each glass.
6. Pour the lemonade cocktail over the ice and add in a lemon and lime and mint sprig for garnish.
7. Serve immediately.

Strawberry Chiffon Pie

This is the pie Howard requested.

TOTAL TIME: Prep: 25 min. + chilling
YIELD: 8 servings.

Ingredients
- 2-1/2 cups sliced fresh strawberries
- 1 envelope unflavored gelatin
- 2 tablespoons lemonade concentrate
- 1/4 cup sugar
- 3 egg whites, lightly beaten
- 1 tablespoon orange juice
- 1-1/2 cups reduced-fat whipped topping
- 1 reduced-fat graham cracker crust (9 inches) or chocolate crumb crust (9 inches)
- 4 large fresh strawberries, halved

Directions
1. Place sliced strawberries in a food processor or blender; cover and process until smooth. Set aside 1-1/2 cups for filling (discard remaining puree or save for another use). In a saucepan, sprinkle gelatin over lemonade concentrate; let stand for 5 minutes. Stir in sugar and reserved strawberry puree. Cook and stir over medium heat until mixture comes to a boil and gelatin is dissolved. Remove from the heat.
2. Stir a small amount of filling into egg whites; return all to the pan, stirring constantly. Cook and stir over low heat for 3 minutes or until the mixture is slightly thickened and a thermometer reaches 160° (do not boil). Remove from the heat; stir in orange juice. Cover and refrigerate for 2 hours, stirring occasionally.
3. Fold in whipped topping; spoon into crust. Cover and refrigerate for 2 hours or until set. Just before serving, garnish with halved strawberries.

The Best Buttermilk-Brined Southern Fried Chicken Recipe

Some of you may remember Donna likes to brine her chicken. My mother always uses an electric skillet to fry hers.

ACTIVE: 45 mins
TOTAL TIME: 5 hrs
YIELD: 3 to 4 servings

Ingredients
- 2 tablespoons paprika
- 2 tablespoons freshly ground black pepper
- 2 teaspoons garlic powder
- 2 teaspoons dried oregano
- 1/2 teaspoon cayenne pepper
- 1 cup buttermilk
- 1 large egg
- Kosher salt
- One whole chicken, about 4 pounds, cut into 10 pieces or 3 1/2 pounds bone-in, skin-on breasts, legs, drumsticks, and/or wings
- 1 1/2 cups all-purpose flour
- 1/2 cup cornstarch
- 1 teaspoon baking powder
- 4 cups vegetable shortening or peanut oil

Directions
1. Combine the paprika, black pepper, garlic powder, oregano, and cayenne in a small bowl and mix thoroughly with a fork.
2. Whisk the buttermilk, egg, 1 tablespoon salt, and 2 tablespoons of the spice mixture in a large bowl. Add the chicken pieces and toss and turn to coat. Transfer the contents of the bowl to a gallon-sized zipper-lock freezer bag and refrigerate for at least 4 hours, and up to overnight, flipping the bag occasionally to redistribute the contents and coat the chicken evenly.
3. Whisk together the flour, cornstarch, baking powder, 2 teaspoons salt, and the remaining spice mixture in a large bowl. Add 3 tablespoons of the marinade from the zipper-lock bag and work it into the flour with your fingertips. Remove one piece of

chicken from the bag, allowing excess buttermilk to drip off, drop the chicken into the flour mixture, and toss to coat. Continue adding chicken pieces to the flour mixture one at a time until they are all in the bowl. Toss the chicken until every piece is thoroughly coated, pressing with your hands to get the flour to adhere in a thick layer.

4. Adjust an oven rack to the middle position and preheat the oven to 350°F. Heat the shortening or oil to 425°F in a 12-inch straight-sided cast-iron chicken fryer or a large wok over medium-high heat. Adjust the heat as necessary to maintain the temperature, being careful not to let the fat get any hotter.

5. One piece at a time, transfer the coated chicken to a fine-mesh strainer and shake to remove excess flour. Transfer to a wire rack set on a rimmed baking sheet. Once all the chicken pieces are coated, place skin side down in the pan. The temperature should drop to 300°F; adjust the heat to maintain the temperature at 300°F for the duration of the cooking. Fry the chicken until it's a deep golden brown on the first side, about 6 minutes; do not move the chicken or start checking for doneness until it has fried for at least 3 minutes, or you may knock off the coating. Carefully flip the chicken pieces with tongs and cook until the second side is golden brown, about 4 minutes longer.

6. Transfer chicken to a clean wire rack set in a rimmed baking sheet, season lightly with salt, and place in the oven. Bake until thickest part of breast pieces registers 150°F (65.5°C) on an instant-read thermometer, and thigh/drumstick pieces register 165°F (74°C), 5 to 10 minutes; remove chicken pieces as they reach their target temperature, and transfer to a second wire rack set in a rimmed baking sheet, or a paper towel-lined plate. Season with salt to taste. Serve immediately—or, for extra-crunchy fried chicken, proceed to step 7.

7. Place the plate of cooked chicken in the refrigerator for at least 1 hour, and up to overnight. When ready to serve, reheat the oil to 400°F. Add the chicken pieces and cook, flipping them once halfway through cooking, until completely crisp, about 5 minutes. Transfer to a wire rack set on a rimmed baking sheet to drain, then serve immediately.

Southern Fried Okra

This is a family favorite, and all credit goes to Pam Duncan.

TOTAL TIME: Prep/Total Time: 30 min.
YIELD: 2 servings.

Ingredients

- 1-1/2 cups sliced fresh or frozen okra, thawed (Fresh is better.)
- 3 tablespoons buttermilk
- 2 tablespoons all-purpose flour
- 2 tablespoons cornmeal
- 1/4 teaspoon salt
- 1/4 teaspoon garlic herb seasoning blend
- 1/8 teaspoon pepper
- Oil for deep-fat frying
- Additional salt and pepper, optional

Directions

1. Pat okra dry with paper towels. Place buttermilk in a shallow bowl. In another shallow bowl, combine the flour, cornmeal, salt, seasoning blend, and pepper. Dip okra in buttermilk, then roll in cornmeal mixture.
2. In an electric skillet or deep-fat fryer, heat 1 in. of oil to 375°. Fry okra, a few pieces at a time, for 1-1/2 to 2-1/2 minutes on each side or until golden brown. Drain on paper towels. Season with additional salt and pepper if desired.

Southern Shrimp and Grits

This wonderful dish can work for breakfast, too. A shout-out to Mandy Rivers for the recipe.

TOTAL TIME: Prep: 15 min. Cook: 20 min.
YIELD: 4 servings.

Ingredients
- 2 cups reduced-sodium chicken broth
- 2 cups 2% milk
- 1/3 cup butter, cubed
- 3/4 teaspoon salt
- 1/2 teaspoon pepper
- 3/4 cup uncooked old-fashioned grits
- 1 cup shredded cheddar cheese

Shrimp:
- 8 thick-sliced bacon strips, chopped
- 1 pound uncooked medium shrimp, peeled and deveined
- 3 garlic cloves, minced
- 1 teaspoon Cajun or blackened seasoning
- 4 green onions, chopped

Directions
1. In a large saucepan, bring the broth, milk, butter, salt, and pepper to a boil. Slowly stir in grits. Reduce heat. Cover and cook for 12-14 minutes or until thickened, stirring occasionally. Stir in cheese until melted. Set aside and keep warm.
2. In a large skillet, cook bacon over medium heat until crisp. Remove to paper towels with a slotted spoon; drain, reserving 4 teaspoons drippings. Sauté the shrimp, garlic, and seasoning in drippings until the shrimp turn pink. Serve with grits and sprinkle with onions.

Cheese Grits & Sausage Breakfast Casserole

A wonderful dish for people who think they don't like grits. Another shout out to Mandy Rivers for the recipe.

TOTAL TIME: Prep: 30 min. Bake: 40 min. + standing
YIELD: 12 servings.

Ingredients
- 2 pounds bulk Italian sausage
- 2 cups water
- 2 cups chicken broth
- 1/2 teaspoon salt
- 1-1/4 cups quick-cooking grits
- 1 pound sharp cheddar cheese, shredded
- 1 cup 2% milk
- 1-1/2 teaspoons garlic powder
- 1 teaspoon rubbed sage
- 6 large eggs, beaten
- Paprika, optional

Directions
1. In a large skillet, cook sausage over medium heat until no longer pink; drain.
2. In a large saucepan, bring the water, broth, and salt to a boil. Slowly stir in grits. Reduce heat; cook and stir for 5-7 minutes or until thickened. Remove from the heat. Add the cheese, milk, garlic powder, and sage, stirring until cheese is melted. Stir in sausage and eggs. Transfer to a greased 13x9-in. baking dish; sprinkle with paprika if desired.
3. Bake, uncovered, at 350° for 40-45 minutes or until a knife inserted in the center comes out clean. Let stand for 10 minutes before serving.

Golden Apple Pie

Many pies go for tart apples, but this one uses Golden Delicious. Thanks, Theresa Brazil, for the recipe.

TOTAL TIME: Prep: 30 min. + cooling Bake: 40 min. + cooling
YIELD: 8 servings.

Ingredients
- 6 cups sliced peeled Golden Delicious apples
- 3/4 cup plus 2 tablespoons apple juice, divided
- 3/4 cup sugar
- 1 teaspoon ground cinnamon
- 1/2 teaspoon apple pie spice
- 2 tablespoons cornstarch
- 1/4 teaspoon vanilla extract

Crust:
- 2-1/2 cups all-purpose flour
- 1 teaspoon salt
- 1 cup cold butter
- 6 to 8 tablespoons ice water

Directions
1. In a large saucepan, combine apples, 3/4 cup apple juice, sugar, cinnamon, and apple pie spice; bring to a boil over medium heat, stirring occasionally. Combine cornstarch and remaining apple juice; add to saucepan. Return to a boil, stirring constantly. Cook and stir 1 minute more or until thickened. Remove from the heat. Stir in vanilla. Cool to room temperature, stirring occasionally.
2. For the crust, combine flour and salt; cut in the butter until the mixture is crumbly. Gradually add water, 1 tablespoon at a time, tossing with a fork until dough can be formed into a ball. Divide into 2 portions, making 1 piece slightly larger. On a lightly floured surface, roll out the larger portion.
3. Line a 9-in. pie plate with bottom crust; trim even with the edge of the plate. Add filling. Roll out remaining dough to fit the top of pie. Place over filling. Trim, seal, and flute edges. Cut slits in top.
4. 4. Bake at 400° for 40-45 minutes or until crust is golden brown and apples are tender. Cool on a wire rack.

Peanut Butter Chocolate Chip Cookies (PBCC Cookies)

A twist on the traditional chocolate chip cookie

YIELD: 25 Servings

Ingredients
- 1/2 cup butter; (1 stick) room temperature
- 1/2 cup shortening
- 1/2 cup creamy peanut butter; resist the temptation to use more
- 1 cup granulated sugar
- 1 cup brown sugar; packed
- 2 1/2 cups regular flour
- 1 1/2 tsp baking soda
- 1 tsp baking powder
- 1/2 tsp salt
- 2 cups chocolate chips; either semi-sweet or milk chocolate

Preparation
1. In a large bowl, mix butter, shortening, peanut butter, granulated and brown sugars, and eggs. If you use a mixer, blend on medium.
2. Separately, mix together flour, baking soda, baking powder, and salt. Add to other mixture. If you use a mixer, start on low speed (don't want to poof flour everywhere!)
3. Mix in chocolate chips.
4. Make large tablespoon-sized balls and lay them out in an airtight container separating each layer with parchment or wax paper.
5. Preheat oven to 400F and place the tablespoon-sized balls onto a cookie sheet lined with Silpat pad or parchment paper.
6. Bake 8 to 10 minutes from room temp, or 12 – 14 minutes from frozen. Time depends a lot on just how big you make them – what you're looking for is a nice golden doneness.
7. Let cool on the cookie sheet

Wedding Cake Blues

THE SWEET, RICH smell of chocolate wafted from the oversized oven, dancing around stainless-steel appliances crammed into the tidy kitchen before slipping into the small waiting area where customers could wait patiently for their morning cup of Joe and a sweet treat. Della Delacroix arched a brow and strained her ears for any jingles of the mounted bell on the entry door indicating incoming or exiting customers. Not a sound—if she discounted her mother humming show tunes. If her mother was humming, it meant no customers. Della closed her eyes and sighed. Her hands settled on her hips as she circled her head, relieving the tension created by her constant downward glance while cooking. Her dark ponytail danced with the action.

Here she was within spitting distance of thirty, working hard to make her dream of owning a bakery a reality. It wasn't a bit like that movie where a guy built a ballpark and all the baseball greats of old came to play. She'd thought it would be enough to bake delicious cakes and pastries at reasonable prices to ensure a thriving business.

Her nose wrinkled, and her top lip curled at her former optimistic outlook about how easy running a bakery would be. The oven buzzer's shrill tone had her hurrying to check her chewy brownie cookies. Timing was everything—too long and they'd be dry. She donned mitts, opened the oven doors, received a blast of heat, and removed the finished cookies.

Her mother, Mabel, strolled into the room, placed her hands on her ample hips, and sniffed the air appreciatively. "Yummy. Gimme a sample."

"No, you don't," Della teased and pivoted, moving the tray of fragrant sweets out of her mother's reach. "Aren't you trying to lose weight for your dating profile pic?"

"Seriously! You act like you don't know me." Mabel jerked her chin upward ruffling her carefully dyed auburn curls. She gestured to her well-proportioned figure. "Haven't you heard men prefer women with a little padding?" A chuckle punctuated her comment before she sighed. "Besides, I think putting up a dating profile is a bit too soon for me." She pointed a manicured finger in Della's direction. "However, not you."

Not this again. It was the twenty-first century, and women could live full lives without marrying and having the usual two children. As a good daughter, Della chose not to mention she wasn't interested in dating. More accurately, she wasn't interested in anyone her mother, her friends, or distant relatives, thought were suitable for her. They never were.

"Mother, it's been seven years since Dad died. He'd want you to be happy."

A snort sounded, and Mabel narrowed her eyes. "If he wanted to make me happy, he would have taken better care of himself, ate better, and exercised."

Mabel waited until the cookie tray went onto the counter before picking up a spatula to lift off a freshly baked cookie. She missed the irony that she just complained about her deceased husband's eating habits while reaching for a calorie-rich goodie. A rapturous expression crossed her face as she chewed.

"This is good!" she declared. With her mouth still full, she reached for another cookie. "Really good."

The praise made Della smile. Compliments on her cooking were always appreciated. "Thanks, Mom. Maybe you could be my testimonial person for an ad. We have to get more people acquainted with our scrumptious fudgy brownie cookies."

"So true." Her mother agreed, giving an emphatic nod while gesturing with a cookie. "There's got to be something we can do. I didn't invest your father's insurance money just to watch it go down the drain."

The words made Della cringe. As the unexpected, only child who showed up as her mother approached forty and had given up all hope of procreating, her mother went out of her way to be the ultimate parent. Della had in no way intended for her cake decorating dreams to suck in her mother, too. Even though she never asked for help, Mabel insisted on forwarding her the money when the bank refused to do so. Businesses failed every day, but Della had no intention of being just another statistic.

She even came up with a cute name, Cupid's Catering Company. Maybe that was a mistake. People who wanted a simple cake, a donut, or even a fast lunch assumed a catering company didn't do basic food. A large wooden sign with the bakery name and tiny chubby cupids with rosy cheeks cavorting on it had cost her plenty. She couldn't afford to change the name on the sign or on her website. Her energy would be better served to concentrate on the catering side.

She took the spatula from her mother and used it to carefully maneuver the chocolate cookies onto lace doilies. "At least we have the McCormick/Lawson wedding coming up."

Mabel mumbled through a full mouth. "Bridezilla." Her accompanying eye-roll filled in the things she didn't say.

Dealing with Ellie McCormick for the last six weeks had not

only added to Della's stress levels but had also caused tension headaches. Ellie had changed the menu at least five times. The upside was Della hadn't ordered too many of the supplies before each change. Other vendors had complained about the difficulty of working with Ellie. It meant it wasn't just Della. This time next month the wedding would be over, and she'd be getting bookings galore from wedding guests. A well-planned catering spread would serve as her audition for future brides and mothers of the brides-to-be.

"Remember! Two hundred of Owens' best people will be the guests."

Mabel snorted. "I've heard that a half-dozen times. You've probably heard it more."

"True." She placed the last cookie on the doily and lifted the tray to carry it into the front area. The breakfast crowd might be slow to non-existent, but their location close to the courthouse had many of the workers stopping in for a quick snack, with the cookies being a favorite.

"All I have to do is grin and bear it. I can handle difficult people as long as they have money in their grubby hands."

She tossed off the last words as she backed into the swinging door that separated the kitchen from the shop area. A slight clearing of a throat had her turning too fast causing the cookies to slide on her tray. Fortunately, she stopped the slide by placing the tray on the counter and smiled at the handsome, bearded man dressed in a pea coat suitable for the chilly, misty weather.

"How can I help you?"

He reached into his wallet, pulled out a ten-dollar bill and flourished it. "I got money in my grubby hand. Hope that means I can get a black coffee and something sweet. Those cookies you almost dropped might do the trick."

"Ah yes."

Color flooded her cheeks. Not only had the man overheard her remark, but he also hadn't hesitated to tease her. Some people might call it flirting. The thought had her crinkling her nose. Men didn't flirt with Della. That much she knew. All through school, her chunky physique earned requests to copy her homework as opposed to dates. Some of the less nice girls referred to her as thunder thighs and plus size nerd.

Once her baking skill emerged right around her junior year, her brownies were another thing in demand. Some mean girls joked she enjoyed her creations—too much. While she felt the need to sample, she didn't gorge herself. Nothing would make her into a waif-thin model. She'd seen the women on her mother's side of the family. Wide hips and generous proportions just happened to be the hand Fate had dealt her.

No reason to flirt back since nothing would come of it. She poured the coffee in a to-go cup without asking if he intended to stay. He struck her as someone who had places to be.

"Sweetheart, I've got a plan to help jumpstart your love life!" her mother called out before pushing the door open and seeing the sole customer. "Oh, sweet pea. I had no clue you were busy."

Somehow, she doubted that. Voices carried, but she hadn't heard the front door bell ring, either. "Not too busy." She smiled at her customer as she handed him the capped cup of coffee.

Her mother plopped her elbow on the counter and rested her chin in her upturned hand. "Hello. You look interesting. Where did you come from?"

Good heavens, not this again. The younger men Mabel chose to chat up probably thought her overfriendly overtures meant cougar city. In truth, her mother was shopping for Della as opposed to herself, which wasn't much better.

Della wrapped the cookie and stuck it into a white bakery bag. "Okay. That will be four dollars and twenty-seven cents."

Bearded and Handsome grinned as he handed over the ten-dollar bill. "Very reasonable. Hope the cookie is as delicious as it smells."

"It is." Some might call her cocky, but she knew her skills, and her fudgy brownie cookies were the best.

"I'll vouch for that," her mother offered and brushed at her mouth to rid herself of any crumbs that might reside. "I didn't catch your name. I thought I knew everyone worth knowing in town."

Would the ground just open and swallow Della? She forced a laugh. "My mom is such a jokester."

She shot her mother a significant look, hoping she'd tone down her attitude. As if expecting this, Mabel turned her head away from Della and focused on the stranger, who grinned at her. He arched an eyebrow, transferred the cookie bag and coffee to his left hand, and stretched out his right hand to Mabel. "I'm Ethan Stone. Pleased to meet you."

Mabel took the offered hand and gave it a hearty shake. "Pleased to meet you, Ethan. I'm Mabel Delacroix. You've already met my daughter, Della."

Ethan nodded convivially, cut his eyes to Della, and then back to Mabel.

Della could almost hear the wheels in his head turning, wondering why anyone would name their daughter Della Delacroix. "Expecting a boy, my parents somehow thought the name they had picked out, Jason, wouldn't serve for a girl."

"I would agree with that."

Her mother sniffed. "You always tell that story in such a judgy way. Please remember I was still under anesthesia. It took a while before I considered that your first name sounded a bit like your last. By then, it was too late."

She waved her hand to rid herself of any condemnation and tsked. "What you must think of us. Don't let me keep you from your big, important job."

He touched a finger to his temple. "I'm the one who should be blushing now. I came here to ask you questions pertinent to my case and ended up buying sweets and chatting. I'm a private investigator."

"What case? What questions?" Unease unfurled in Della's stomach like one of those resurrection plants you add water to, and they miraculously come to life. Her water tended to be the unknown and uncertain, which often were the same.

"Jeffrey Lawson. Have you seen him lately?" The words hung in the air, changing the former light-hearted atmosphere.

As the potential groom of Bridezilla, Della had seen him squirm as Ellie complained about how provincial their sample menus were. A dazed look had settled on him when Ellie changed the menu for the fourth time. Most of the time, the well-groomed heir to Lawson Industries acted as if he'd rather be anywhere else other than listening to his fiancée rage against the world and threaten financial as well as legal repercussions if she wasn't satisfied.

"Well, I have seen him. Maybe a week ago. He was with Ellie."

Ethan shook his head and grimaced. "Not good. You were the last wedding vendor I've contacted. I hoped you might know something the others didn't. Thanks, anyhow."

His brow furrowed as he worked out whatever issue was troubling him. Both Mabel and Della held up a hand in farewell, but he never even noticed. Ethan exited, clutching his bakery bag and coffee.

Della waited until the door closed before speaking. "Now I'm worried there might not be a wedding. The man probably hightailed it after the fourth menu change."

"Could be," her mother agreed. "It's more likely his family had him kidnapped to prevent the nuptials."

Out of the two of them, Della considered her thought to be the more practical one. Only this time, her mother might be right.

Even though it might be selfish on her part, she needed this wedding. After insisting the menu couldn't be changed again, Ellie McCormick had agreed to the final menu. However, Bridezilla could still try.

"There's only one thing we can do—find Jeffrey Lawson."

Her mother rested one hand on her hip and regarded her daughter with disbelief. "How are we supposed to do that? It seems to me Ethan is doing that now, and he doesn't sound like he's having much luck. Why would *we* succeed when he hasn't?"

Normally, she'd be the naysayer, but she *needed* to cater this event and earn the money it provided. Della walked over to her mother and hooked arms with hers. "We make a great team in the bakery and out. We are not without skills. Didn't we both live with one of the county's best detectives?"

"Your father was second to none." A smile danced across her mother's face as her eyes rolled upward, remembering. "Still," she gave a slight sniff, "Owens is far from big city crime. Many of the crimes he solved were partially due to information gathered from my gossip hotline."

Her mother tapped her head, reminiscent of how her father had done and lowered her voice to imitate the man. "Fred Lowenstein is missing his brand-new Mercury sedan. Who does your gossip hotline like for it?"

"Dad couldn't arrest someone based on gossip!" The revelation that her father had asked her mother for local gossip stunned, but she knew from her obsession with crime dramas and mysteries that the casual observer knew a great deal.

"No, he didn't arrest them on gossip." Mabel's crow's feet gathered at the corners of her eyes as she chuckled, making her resemble a cheerful gnome minus the beard. "He checked them out, did the legwork, and sometimes the gossip proved right. If nothing else, it was a good starting point. The person of interest usually threw someone else under the bus." Her shoulders went up in a shrug. "In the end, your father got his man, or in some cases, woman. I think he may have thought you'd follow in his footsteps."

Memories of donning one of her father's cast-off suit jackets and brandishing an oversized magnifying glass when she was ten took shape in her mind. Her father used to call her his junior detective and even give her missions to find things. Usually, it was objects such as missing car keys, tickets to an upcoming baseball game, or the remote he had misplaced and, on a few occasions, he even laid out clues for her to decipher. It boosted her confidence in her investigative skills so much that she volunteered to discover who had helped themselves to the money from the scout bake sale.

The troop's original intention had been to give the money to the local animal shelter. Della deduced the possible thief was also her fellow scout at the time, the only one left alone with the money who suddenly had a large supply of junk food she hadn't brought with her. Rather than turn her in, Della managed to convince the girl to return the money minus the six dollars or so she'd already spent at the nearby convenience store. The incident ended her love of investigation and scouting.

The other scouts and leaders assumed she was the culprit. Despite knowing her and how hard she worked for the troop, they immediately fingered her for the crime, which made her want nothing to do with them in the future. Of course, her parents wanted to intervene, but Della wanted none of it. The light-fingered scout stayed in the troop and possibly gossiped about the incident, naming Della as the thief.

While she might not have said the actual words, Della swore off all investigative pursuits after experiencing the way they could come back and bite you. Now, though, if she didn't do something, her hopes and dreams would blow up like her scouting efforts.

"Dad was the best," Della admitted, returning to the conversation. She crossed her arms and leaned against the counter. "That doesn't mean everyone else is stellar."

"Have to admit, I've never found anyone as special as him."

Della arched her eyebrows over the comment. As far as she knew, her parent hadn't even considered dating, let alone remarriage. "I assume you're talking about detective work as opposed to husband."

"Both," her mother corrected and turned away.

Now, she'd gone and made her mother cry. Whenever she turned away like that, it was to hide a tear. Time to change the subject or at least steer it away from her father. She pushed off the counter. "I've read most people assume everyone else thinks like they do or works as hard as they do. That's why they're puzzled by those who don't."

Her mother turned, her mascara smudged at the corner of her right eye. Forcing a smile, she asked, "This is leading where?"

"We assume everyone we meet works as hard as we do. What if

they don't? Come on, think about it. You've got plenty of people bragging about how they graduated at the top of their class, which may or may not be true. Some of us must have lawyers, doctors, accountants, etc., who graduated at the bottom of their class."

Mabel held out her hand, palm out in a halt gesture. "I'd rather not think about that." Her nose crinkled. "Makes me uneasy. Are you saying half our town isn't any good at their professions?"

"Maybe not half. Some of those bottom of the classers moved elsewhere. You have to admit some are better than others." She waited for her mother to acknowledge that with a head bob. "This goes for any profession. Maybe Ethan looks the part, but he doesn't have the investment we do in locating Lawson. Let him do his thing. We do ours. As far as tracking a missing man, you've got a gossip hotline second to none that can throw light on why the man is nowhere to be found."

Her mother sniffed. "I may be good, but it doesn't take a genius to understand why Lawson is making himself scarce. He's found himself hogtied to Ellie McCormick. I'd chew my leg off to get away."

Della held up her hand. "You have a point, but it has to be more than that. Why hire an investigator? We need to find out why the man ran off? Or even whom the man ran off *to*? Or where?"

Her mother's expression morphed from doubtful to curious. "That does sound up my alley. What's your role?"

"Analytical, of course. We know why he ran—mostly. I need to figure out how to allay his fears, get him back, and save our event." Even though her words were bold, Della had no clue how it would work, but work it had to since this was her first wedding catering job.

"Count me in!" her mother chimed.

Author Notes

The Painted Lady Inn Mysteries is my first cozy mystery series. My husband and I concocted the premise when I was penning romances for a different publisher. The main character, Donna, is heavily based on my mother, but my husband swears he sees a lot of me in her. I guess it shouldn't be too surprising because I was always a mystery buff. From a young age, my grandmother used to call me the *Why Girl* because I always wanted to know the *why* behind everything. It wasn't enough to know something just *was*. Even though I was a fan of *Unsolved Mysteries*, I still needed that update when they caught the culprit and discovered the motivation.

This has led me to binge-watch police dramas, BBC mysteries, and listen to cold case podcasts. I'm also a killer Clue player, but my biggest research tool is people watching. With the pandemic, I have to do this from a distance. While out in public, I've overheard many an interesting conversation including one where a woman solicited help in securing a GPS device underneath her husband's car to track his movements.

Ironically, I've had three incidents where I knew or even taught the killer. Personally, I like to keep the murders fictional. ☺

Hope you enjoy **Two Many Sleuths** and the many down-home recipes. For those who wonder about my roots, although not born south of the Mason Dixon line, I did live in Charleston, South Carolina for a while and vacationed in Duck, North Carolina. This explains all the frequent trips to Asheville and Charleston my characters take. Some of my favorite memories of Charleston include the Isle of the Palms beach and the Battery with its pastel-painted houses.

I love to hear from and meet readers. In the meantime, stay in touch via my newsletter. Sign up at www.morgankwyatt.com. Subscribers to my newsletter find out about exclusive freebies, contests, and personal appearances.

If you feel like writing a review, please do.

Reading takes you to your happy place. We need happy moments now more than ever.

MK Scott
www.morgankwyatt.com

www.ingramcontent.com/pod-product-compliance
Lightning Source LLC
Chambersburg PA
CBHW020907180626
46816CB00007BA/2275